"James Sallis breathes new life into the wheezing detective genre with Lew Griffin, a black resident of the seamier side of New Orleans. . . . Griffin is an original creation, a loner who, in the classic private eye tradition, does things his own way, in his own time."
— *San Francisco Chronicle*

"Sallis is, simply, the best writer of the existential mystery now writing it, and maybe the best existential novelist of our times."
— *Mystery News*

"Sallis has cooked up an intoxicating mixture in Lew Griffin, a black private eye operating in the Big Easy. . . . If you're tired of boilerplate potboilers, dip into James Sallis for a refreshingly literate mystery."
— *The Charlotte Observer*

"Sallis is one of the least conventional and most interesting writers working in the mystery genre."
— *Publishers Weekly*

"James Sallis is a fine writer with sheer artistry in his painting of word pictures."
— *The News-Sentinal* (Fort Wayne, IN)

"No private eye can compete in the philosophy department with Lew Griffin, the creation of poet, essayist, and novelist James Sallis."
— *San Jose Mercury News*

BLUEBOTTLE

ALSO BY JAMES SALLIS

FICTION
The Long-Legged Fly (1992)
Moth (1993)
Black Hornet (1994)
Eye of the Cricket (Walker and Company, 1997)
A Few Last Words (1970)
Limits of the Sensible World (1994)
Renderings (1995)

NONFICTION
The Guitar Players (1982, 1994)
Difficult Lives (1993)

AS EDITOR
The Shores Beneath (1971)
The War Book (1972)
Jazz Guitars (1984)
The Guitar in Jazz (1996)
Ash of Stars: On the Writing of Samuel R. Delany (1996)

AS TRANSLATOR
Saint Glinglin by Raymond Queneau (1993)

FORTHCOMING
Gently into the Land of the Meateaters (essays)
Chester Himes: A Life (biography)

BLUEBOTTLE

A LEW GRIFFIN NOVEL

James Sallis

WALKER & COMPANY

New York

First published in the United States of America in 1999 by Walker Publishing Company, Inc.;
first paperback edition published in 2000.

Published simultaneously in Canada by Fitzhenry and Whiteside, Markham, Ontario L3R 4T8

The poem on pages 18–19, "Wise 3" by Amiri Baraka, was originally published in *Transbluesency: The Selected Poems of Amiri Baraka / LeRoi Jones.* Copyright 1995 Marsilio Publishers and Amiri Baraka. Used by permission.

Library of Congress Cataloging-in-Publication Data
Sallis, James
Bluebottle: a Lew Griffin novel/James Sallis.
p. cm.
ISBN 0-8027-3323-9
PS3569.A462B54   1998
813'.54—dc21   98-25648
CIP
ISBN 0-8027-7595-0 (paperback)

Series design by Mauna Eichner

Printed in Canada
2   4   6   8   10   9   7   5   3   1

To Gordon Van Gelder

Same vineyard, different grapes

And I am lost in the beautiful white ruins
Of America.

—James Wright

In justice to my father, one should note that
he resorted to elaborate invention only after
first experimenting with simple falsehood.

— Machado de Assis

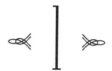

e still, sir—" Her head turned away. "Anyone get his name?"

From across the room: "Lewis Griffin."

"Be still, Mr. Griffin. Please. Work with us here. We know the pain's bad."

I formed a slurry of words that failed to make it from mind to tongue, then tried again, something simpler: "Yes." When I was a kid we'd practice doo-wop songs in the tile bathroom at school. That's what my voice sounded like.

"I can give you something to help." She spoke across me, someone at the other side of the gurney. Gobbledy, gobbledy, fifty milligobbles.

"There. Should start easing off pretty quickly. . . . Better?"

"Mmm." Was it? My voice feathery now, floating. Not that the pain had gone away or diminished, but I didn't care anymore. I turned my head. Sideways room the size of a dancehall. Glare everywhere. Someone on the next stretcher was dying with great ceremony and clamor, half a dozen staff in attendance. I saw tears running down one nurse's face. She looked to be in her early twenties.

"You've been shot, Mr. Griffin. We can't be sure just how serious it is, not yet. Bear with us. Can you feel this?"

Something ran up the sole of my right foot, then the left.

"Yes."

"And this?"

Pinpricks on both hands. First one, a pause, then two, like Morse. A tattoo, drummers would call it. Tattoo needles. Queequeg. Fiji islanders. Gauguin in Tahiti, those brown bodies. Tattoo of rain on the roof.

"Mr. Griffin?"

"Mmm."

"I asked could you feel that."

"Yes ma'am." But I felt a tug towards something else, something other—body and mind borne on separate tides, about to wash up on separate shores.

"Super. Okay, Jody, let's get blood work. ABG, SMAC, type and crossmatch from the way it's looking. X-ray's on the way, right?"

"So they tell us."

Meanwhile connections between myself and the world were faltering, as though tiny men with hatchets hacked away at cables linking us, cables that carried information, images, energy, power. The world, what I could see of it, had contracted to a round tunnel, through which I sighted. On the rim, just out of sight, images sparked and fell away into darkness. Beautiful in the way only lost things can be. Then darkness closed its hand.

"Music."

"What?"

She leaned close.

"Music. There, behind all the rest." Like the sound of your body coming up around you deep in the night, creaking floorboards, snap and buzz of current within walls, this singing in wires a house, a body, requires.

Nietzsche said that without music life would be a mistake. Danny Barker breathed it in and out like air. Or Buddy Bolden: carried through slaughter to cut hair at the state hospital, remembering all his life how once he'd banged the bell of his horn on the floor and got the whole town's attention. Walter Pater.

"He's hearing the Muzak overhead," someone said.

What all art aspires to, the condition of.

"That's an old Lonnie Johnson tune," I told them.

"I can't see," I said.

Suddenly she was close again and I smelled her breath, tatters of perfume and sweat, suggestion of menstrual blood, as she leaned above me.

"Tell me when you see the light, when it goes away." As the world has done. "Mr. Griffin?"

I shook my head. "Sorry."

"Jody, I want a CAT scan. *Now*. Radiology tries stalling, anyone up there even clears his throat, you let me know."

World rendered down to sound, sensation. Rebuild it from this, what will I get? Fine word, *render*, bursting at the seams. Render unto Caesar. A court chef reports: forty choice hams for rendering to stock. Deliver, give up, hand down judgment, restore. Reproduce or represent by artistic or verbal means.

A Cajun waltz with seesaw accordion replaced Lonnie

Johnson overhead. Tug of the stretcher's plastic against my skin, slow burn at the back of my hand where there's a needle and drugs course in. Coppery smell of fresh blood. Layers of voices trailing off into the distance. New horizons everywhere.

Now with a lurch brakes are kicked off and we're barreling headfirst, headlong. Past patchworks of conversations, faces above, curious sounds. Through automatic doors that snap open like a soldier's salute, along hallways smelling of disinfectant, onto an elevator.

Down.

I think of Emily Dickinson's "Before I had my eye put out." Remember both Blind Willies, Blind Lemon, Riley Puckett. Maybe they'll teach me to play.

Down.

Wonder if Milton's waiting down there to give me a few tips. Friends call him Jack, wife and daughters attend his every need.

I WAS TRYING to read a book but the damned thing kept talking to me, interrupting. Don't turn this page, it would say. Or: You don't have any idea what this is all about, where I'm going with this, do you. Gotcha. You don't know the real me at all. Look, no hands!

One hand, at least.

It rested lightly on my shoulder.

"Just like home, huh, Lew. Sound asleep at three in the afternoon."

I started to grunt, but it hurt so much I didn't carry through. Those same little men who'd hacked through the cables connecting world and self had sneaked in while I slept and glued my tongue to the top of my mouth. It came loose, finally, with a tearing sound.

"You started smoking again. Pizza for lunch. Laundry's piling up."

Holmes had nothing on me. Other senses more acute and all that.

"Amazing. Absolutely amazing."

I knew he'd be shaking his head.

"Only the smell's soaked up from the department, which you'll remember is pretty much an ashtray fitted with desks and file cabinets. Pizza, right—but for breakfast, not lunch. Been in the fridge awhile. I *think* the green was peppers."

"Keep the faith."

"Not to mention the leftovers. Exactly. And I'm wearing new pants because my old ones don't fit anymore. I finally broke down, bought new ones."

Four or five pair all the same, if I knew Don. He shopped (an event taking place every decade or so) the way frontiersmen laid in provisions. Staples. In quantity.

"They've got that smell they always have. Cleaning fluids or whatever."

"Yeah, guess they do."

"You could always wash them first."

"*Before* I wear them?" His tone sprinkled salts of incredulity over the concept. File with Flat Earth, maybe. Or the wit and wisdom of Richard Nixon. "I don't know, Lew. Way too much time sitting behind a desk filling out paperwork, humping the phone. Ever since I came off patrol and started wearing these monkey suits. I see the street, it's out the window, like some painting, you know? Hanging on the wall. Hung up there myself."

I heard him sink into the chair alongside. One chair leg was short. He eased his weight off and moved the chair around, trying for better topography.

"So how you doing?"

"Hell if I know. Have to ask the experts."

"I did. Just came from a long talk with Dr. Shih. She's pretty sure the blindness is temporary. Happens sometimes with major trauma, she says. They don't know why."

She proved to be right. In following weeks sight returned by increments. Veil after veil fell away. Light swelled slowly till I was aware of its presence. Then light became motion, mass, outline, form—at last shaped itself again into the world I knew, or something close enough.

"You remember my being here before?"

I shook my head.

"I've been by every day. It's Thursday. You were brought in over a week ago. We've had conversations, some of them truly strange. One time you went on for better than an hour about Roshomon and Ahab's gold sovereign. Then you had to tell me about some book called *Skull Meat*. Plot, characters, what the neighborhood looked like. Set over in Algiers. Couldn't tell whether you were supposed to have read it or written it, that kind of wobbled back and forth. Told me the book's hero finally got fed up with the whole thing and walked out—right off the page. Now that's a *real* hero, you said."

"Must be the drugs they were giving me."

"Yeah. Must be."

"The part about the character stalking off's stolen from Queneau, of course."

"Of course."

Don shifted again in his chair. Any moment, things

can fall on you, disappear from under you. What you hope, all you hope, is that the seat you're on just now's a safe one.

"Shih asked me about your drinking, Lew. Halfway through the operation you started waking up from the anesthetic. Shih says people only do that when their bodies are accustomed to high levels of depressives."

A bird alit (I guessed from the sound) on the sill outside, then with a sudden whir of wings was gone. Shadow of the waxwing slain by the false azure of the windowpane.

"I know it's been bad. Maybe some of it has to do with what happened up there in Baton Rouge. God knows what else. Maybe it's worse than either of us thought. Maybe someday we oughta sit down and talk about it."

We were quiet for a time then.

"LaVerne's been here too, you know, two, three times a day."

Sudden aromatic assault as he took the lid off a cup of *café au lait*.

"One for you," holding it out, waiting as my hand groped and made contact. I pushed up in bed, against the headboard. Heard him peel the lid off another cup. He blew across its mouth. The smell grew stronger.

"Shih says you shouldn't worry over the gaps for now. That some memories may come back in distorted form or not at all, but that most *will* come back, and for the most part whole."

There were memories, parts of my life, I wouldn't have minded losing, even back then. Don knew that's what I was thinking.

"Verne's okay?"

"Sure she is. Worried about you, like the rest of us."

We were quiet again. I imagined Don looking off the way he did, watching nothing in particular.

"You remember what happened, Lew?"

I shook my head. "Pieces. Fragments that don't fit together. Images. Some of what I *do* remember seems more like a dream than anything real."

"You met a woman in a bar downtown, said she was a journalist."

Random moments surfaced. Denim skirt, silk jacket. One eye peering at me through a glass of Scotch. Glass none too clean and Scotch raw as rubbing alcohol: *that* kind of bar.

"You stayed there just over three hours. Buster Robinson was playing. Lady's got a taste for the music, it seems. Taste for something, anyway. Last month or so, she'd made herself a regular down there along Poydras."

"But not before."

"So far as we can tell, nobody ever saw her before that. Nor will any newspaper for a hundred miles around lay claim to her."

We sipped *café au lait*.

"Between you you threw back close to thirty dollars' worth. She tried to put it on American Express and they just looked at her. Get serious, you know? Wound up giving them a fifty and said keep the change."

"Wanted to make sure she was remembered."

"As though a white woman down there wouldn't be already, yeah. The two of you left together then, most likely to get something to eat. Barmaid heard you talking about Ye Olde College Inn and Dunbar's. The name Eddie B. also came up a couple of times, she says. You told this Esmay woman you had to make one quick stop first."

"I was meeting Eddie Bone."

"That's how we figure it."

"Why would I do that? *No one* looks for Eddie Bone."

"Yeah, people've been known to leave town to avoid looking for him."

Holding the cup two-handed, I dropped an index finger to measure liquid level, brought the cup to my face, cautiously sipped.

"Give it time, Lew. You're just gonna have to pull back here all around, give things room to happen."

"And hope they do."

He must have nodded, then caught himself. "Yeah," he said.

"You'd barely stepped outside when the shots came. Couple of kids from the cleaners next door were in the alley out back on a break, passing joints and a bottle of George Dickel back and forth. They tell us you two came out the front door and stood there a minute talking, then you stepped around and embraced her. One of them remembers saying Now *that's* something you ain't gonna see uptown and handing the bottle over. Then the shots came. Guy reaching for the bottle dropped it."

I sipped coffee again. Sartre's got this long rap in *Being and Nothingness* about smoking in the dark, how different the experience becomes. In my own dark now, I was forced to admit this was one time he seemed to be onto something. Ordinary coffee, the drinking of it, had become a kind of sacrament. Visual clues missing, true. Sartre pointed out one's inability to see the smoke, to observe one's own breath course in and out. But whatever the loss, there was greater gain: the physical world, its smells, its heats and anticipations, fell upon you with unsuspected intensity.

"The shots were meant for her," I said.

Don's chair creaked.

"It's a possibility we've considered."

Finishing my coffee, I set the cup on the bedside table and heard Don's empty cup click down beside it. A group of visitors or new employees passed as though on tour at a museum in the hall outside. A young man with a voice like a rapidly dripping faucet guided them, pointing out the hospital's various departments and unique services.

"We haven't had any luck tracking her down. Maybe she's gone to ground, scared of what almost happened." Don shifted again in his chair. "For all we know, maybe it was just coincidence."

"Or a setup."

"Yeah. Have to tell you the thought crossed my mind. Mine and some others' as well. Then, the morning after this shooter takes you down, Eddie Bone himself turns up dead. He's got this room all set up at home, must be eight, ten thousand dollars' worth of gym equipment in there. Squad responding to an anonymous call finds him slumped over the handlebars of his exercise bike, naked. They figure at first it's a heart attack, something like that, but then they see something hanging out of his mouth. When they raise his head they find a dead rat crammed in his mouth."

"Cute."

"You bet. One thing these guys have, it's a sense of humor. We didn't wonder what the connection was before, how Bone and this woman fit, where it all came from, now we have to."

With a sketchy knock the door eased open to concatenations of horns, whistles and buzzers from the lounge TV, someone winning a load on a game show. No music up here. Just this gabble of America's threadbare culture.

"Mr. Griffin. You've a visitor. From New York, he says."

My visitor from New York came in limping. Maybe he'd walked all the way. The side of one shoe dragged as he approached.

A year and spare change later, four A.M. on a Sunday, my phone would ring for Lee's wife to tell me that, waking and turning Leewards that morning, she'd found him dead. Lee's diabetes had been out of control for some time, she said—remember how his feet always hurt? I hung up the phone, lay back down alongside LaVerne and held her close.

"Mr. Griffin? Thanks for seeing me."

A pause.

"Lee Gardner."

A longer pause. I realized that he'd put his hand out, reached till I found it, and shook.

"Poor choice of words, perhaps, in the circumstance. I had no idea of your situation, of course. No, wait. I need to back up here, don't I? Marvelous thing, time's elasticity. Though I suppose it always slaps into you on the snapback. Like Thurber's claw of the seapuss, gets us all in the end. I've just come from the police. A detective there gave me your name. But that's still not the place to start, is it. Sorry. And it's all mutable. Once an editor . . . I've already told you my name. I come from Maine. Taking care of all that David Copperfield business, right?

"I'm an editor at Icarus Books. Editor-publisher, actually. One of our authors, R. Amano—you may know of his work, his novel about Gilles de Rais started at the top of the best-seller list and sank slowly through it a few years back—lives here in the city. In, if you can believe it, a house trailer that once belonged to his parents. Says there's nothing he treasures more than that view of the woods on one side and, on the other, the gravel parking lot of a country-music juke joint.

"Now Hollywood wants to buy one of his books, not the Gilles de Rais, the one we thought would be a sure shot, *Bury All Towers*, but another one, this tiny little novel about a man on death row awaiting execution and another who comes out of a ten-year coma, been out of print twelve years at least. Ray doesn't have an agent and asked me to negotiate the contract for him, which I did. But then all of a sudden Ray stopped answering his mail. We call, this man who seldom steps outside the trailer, rolls from bed to the kitchen counter where he works and back to bed, with time out maybe for a sandwich and three pots of coffee, he's never home. I send telegrams— no response. Meanwhile the producer's calling us up two, three times a week. We tell him we're on top of it, naturally.

"Sorry. I've rather torn into it here, haven't I? Forever leaping into things. Always saying sorry too, come to think of it. Mother was an actress. Grand entrances all her life. And spent most of her life apologizing, trying to explain away her regrets.

"What she really was was one of the first rock-and-rollers, sang background for an awful lot of those late-Fifties, Dell Shannon, Dion, Brian Hyland things. But all her life she insisted on actress, which was the way she'd started out."

Don and I waited. New York seemed to have run down.

"Pleased to meet you, Mr. Gardner," I said.

Don grunted. I could have told you within inches, just from the sound, where he was. "Guess I better get on downtown. Shift changes in a couple hours and we're half a dozen men short as usual." He'd been put on the desk while recuperating from a near-fatal gunshot, kept there because with him at the helm, for the first time in years the ship failed to run aground. He hated it. "Later, Lew."

The door fanned open and shut to the sound of recycling laughter.

"You're not up to this, I need to leave, just tell me," Gardner said.

"Company's appreciated. No extra points for distance, though."

"Distance is easy. A thing I'm good at."

"We all have our strengths."

Was there, then, another rustle of wings at the window? A sound like LaVerne's satin dresses or gown.

"People out there in the lobby watching, whatsit, *Days of Our Lives*," Gardner said. "Doctors playing back tapes they'd made secretly months ago when everyone believed Sylvia was dying and husband Dean sat there day after day telling her 'all the things I've never told *anyone*.' Now Sylvia's made this miraculous recovery and it's—organ chord—Truth Time. My mother used to watch that show."

"Lots did. And still do."

"Not exactly Dostoevski or Dickens."

"Not even Irwin Shaw."

"But it's all we have. What we live with."

I listened to my visitor's foot drag towards the window. He pulled the window open. I was surprised this proved possible in such a building. But yes, there were sudden new tides of air, smell, sound.

"Maybe what people are starting to say, is true. Maybe what those like myself do, everything we believe in—literature, fine music, fine writing, the arts generally—maybe none of that matters anymore. We're digging up ruins. Quaint as archaeologists."

"I assume your Mr. Amano doesn't write soap operas."

Gardner laughed. "Actually, now that you mention it, he *did* for a while a few years back. Paid the rent, bought groceries, kept (as he said) slim body and slimmer soul together. Not something he wants remembered. And they were exceedingly *strange* soap operas.

"But I've gotten astray of any point, haven't I? Sorry.

"There's that word again.

"Mountain and Mohammed time, I finally decided. Flew in from New York, picked up a rental car and drove out to Kingfisher Mobile Home Park. The door to fourteen-D was open, naturally. Ray told me he had no idea where the key was. TV on inside, sound turned down, some old movie, flickers of light. Four plates, rinsed but far from clean, stacked by the side of the sink. Carry-out cartons in the trash, also a package of chicken awrithe with maggots beneath the wrapping. Dozen or so empty beer bottles lined against the back wall by the sink. Books everywhere."

"And no writer."

"No writer." For some reason I imagined Gardner's fingers moving about independently as he spoke, seeking phones to dial, yet-unbreached manuscripts, a desktop with objects wanting rearrangement, and thought of Nerval's disembodied hand, Cendrars's *main coupée*, *Beast with Five Fingers*. "I went immediately to the police, of course. They didn't want to hear about it. When I insisted, they filled out report forms. Told me there wasn't much they'd be able to do beyond getting this information out. I sat there drinking bad coffee and not doing the one thing they most wanted me to do, which was to go away. So finally they offered a private detective's number, said maybe I'd want to get in touch with him."

"A. C. Boudleaux." Achilles. Ah-*sheel*.

"The same. I finally track him down to this café the size of a railroad car on the edge of town, built out over water like steaming green soup. Looks like the place's been around long enough for Longfellow to have sat in there writing *Evangeline*. Boudleaux listens, then tells me 'No pun intended, but I'm swamped.' Gives me *your* number. 'Missing persons, you won't find anyone better.' When I call the number Boudleaux gave me, a young lady answers, tells me you're here."

"Given the circumstances, I don't see how I can help you, Mr. Gardner."

"Of course. But the circumstances were exactly what I didn't know. *Now* I don't know why I've gone on so about all this."

When he stood I sensed a change in light. Something moved towards me. His hand again. I found it, shook.

"Good luck to you, Mr. Griffin."

"And to you."

He went out the door. Not much by way of sound out there now. Hall lights bright like a sea around the dark, dark island of his form.

. . .

THAT NIGHT LAVERNE stopped by on her way to work with a cassette player and a recording of black poets reading their work.

"Something I thought you might like, Lew."

I did. And must have listened to it thirty or forty times over the next several days. Something about being cut off from the visual world made that tape so much more *real* to me, so much more substantial. I began living in those words and voices—living through them.

LaVerne had heard the album, from a New York label that put out a steady stream of Southern field recordings, folk music by aging Trotskyites and suburban youngsters, klezmer, polka, at a client's home.

"Thanks."

My arms went out and she was there, in them.

"You smell good."

"I won't for long. Seven at night and it still has to be a hundred degrees out there."

"You could take the night off."

"And do what? You just get yourself well and come home. *Then* I'll take the night off. Maybe several nights."

"You mean like a date?"

"Yeah." Whenever she focused on something close, her eyes seemed to cross. It gave her face a vulnerable, softly sexy look. Broke my heart every time. I couldn't see her then, but I knew she was doing it. "Yeah, like a date, Lewis."

She stretched out on the bed beside me, smoothed her dress back under her. Neither of us spoke for a while.

I don't remember this, of course. Verne told me about it later, some of it. The rest, I imagined into place.

"It's been a while since we did this, Verne."

Turning, she tucked her head against my arm. I felt the warmth of her breath on my chest as she spoke.

"I miss you, Lew. Miss you sometimes even when you're there. But I miss you a whole lot more when you're gone."

I don't know how long we lay like that. Once a nurse started peremptorily into the room, fetched up stock-still just inside the door and backed out without a word.

When LaVerne sat up, the fabric of her satin dress crackled. She wore her hair long then, cut straight across front and back.

"Maybe this is different from most of life, Lewis. Maybe this is something we can fix."

I put my hand on her waist.

After a moment she stood. Began tucking things in. Breast, hair, slip. Her sadness.

"Have to go, Lew. Late enough start as it is."

"If it's as hot as you say it is, things'll be slow on the street."

"You never know. Sometimes heat just brings the beast out."

"Take care. . . ." She was almost to the door. "Verne?"

A pause. "Yeah, Lew."

"Is it dark outside?"

That's what bothered me most. Where things were, the shapes of rooms, finding my way to toilet and lavatory—all minor problems. But being suspended in time, out of the gather and release of the day, was something else entirely, an immeasurable loss.

"Almost," she said.

"A clear night?"

"Pinpricks of stars in the upper window. Moon will be full in another day or two."

"And city lights stretched out below us."

"Yes."

"Diminutive fires of the planet, Neruda called them."

"Sure he did. See you tomorrow, hon."

I remembered lines from a Langston Hughes poem: Night comes slowly, black like me. Once LaVerne was gone, I nudged tape into player. Sure enough, Hughes's poem was there, right after one about a lynching. Further along was another, by LeRoi Jones / Amira Baraka, that would haunt me for years.

Son singin
fount some
words. Son
singin
in that other

language
talkin bout "bay
bee, why you
leave me
here," talkin bout
"up under de sun
cotton in my hand." Son
singing, think he bad
cause he
can speak
they language, talkin bout
"dark was the night
the ocean deep

white eyes cut through me
made me weep."

Son singin
fount some words. Think
he bad. Speak
they
language.
'sawright
I say
'sawright
wit me

look like
yeh, we gon be here
a taste.

I think that may have been the first time I thought
about all these different languages we use. Danny Barker
used to talk about that, how with this group of musicians
he'd talk one way, that way with another one, uptown and
downtown talk, and still he'd have this private language
he'd use at home, among friends. We all do that. To survive, our forebears learned dissimulation and mimickry,
learned never to say what they truly thought. They knew
they were gon be here a taste. That same masking remains
in many of us, in their children's blood, a slow poison. So
many of us no longer know who, or what, we are.

er hair had come out of a bottle. So had courage, gait and gestures. But somehow it was all of a piece; it worked.

"Hope you don't mind if I tell you you're a good-looking man," she said as she sat down beside me. She'd successfully crossed troubled seas between her seat at the bar and my table, listing but slightly starboard. Now here was this new challenge: a fair distance (as my father would have said) from up there to down here. Heroically she made it.

Matter of fact, I didn't mind at all. A lot of my own life was coming out of a bottle those days. This white woman made her hobby drinking bad whiskey and picking up bad company in cheap bars, what business was it of mine. Lord knows I'd fished often enough in *her* pond.

Never question what Providence spills in your lap.

She wanted Scotch and got it. Sat swirling it around in her glass the way stone drinkers do that first hit or two, savoring color, body, bouquet, legs, letting those first sips roll across the back of her tongue, equal parts anticipation and relief. Before long she'd be slamming it back. Not tasting it at all, just letting it take her where she needed to be. Before long, too, her conversation would start to narrow, go round and round in circles like someone lost in the woods. I knew. But for the time being she lay warm and safe in the bosom of that wonderland alcohol grants its acolytes, a zone where, for a short time at least, everything fell back into place, everything made some kind of sense.

When I was a kid my mom would drape these pinned-together cutout paper patterns for clothes she was sewing us over the kitchen table. She only did that when I was very young and soon gave it up—just as she gave up most everything else. But I loved sitting there looking at those patterns: some kind of thin, opaque paper you saw nowhere else, pins holding it together, half on the table and half off. Destined soon for the trash; but briefly it pulled one small part of the world together, gave it rare form.

Dana, she said, shaking hands rather more fiercely than the situation called for. A journalist. Wrote a column for one of the local papers. Maybe I'd even seen it. Society stuff mostly, who was seen where wearing what in the company of whom and where they'd all gone to school, leaning on connections an uptown family, a couple of society marriages and her Newcomb degree gave her. But now and again, hanging out in bars like this one or dredging her way through the Quarter, The Seven Seas, Lafitte's, La Casa, she'd get on to something hard.

Hard *news*, she meant.

I remember—or imagine—or I dreamed—her leaning across the table, breasts pushing up towards her blouse's undone top button as they came to rest on the tabletop.

You understand, Lewis?

Guess I did.

But I had to wonder how provisional *all* our understanding is, finally. Look, I told her: I'm a black man, still young. You're a white woman, what, halfway along in life? We've come up in different worlds. Hell, we *exist* in different worlds. Always will. You think there's some secret passage behind the bookcase like in old movies, lets us get from one to the other?

Felt for a moment like I was back at UNO, one of those embarrassingly intense late-night sessions debating such topics as the problem of evil, whether to order pizza or burgers, and whether black folks had souls.

"What I think there are," she said, "are doors. We only have to choose to—" Her hand made the gesture of reaching out to push a door open, hesitated, then fell on mine.

"In and out of lots of doors, are you, then?"

She nodded. "Had a few slammed behind me, too."

"Bet you have."

Then—seemingly without transition—we were talking about King Lear.

I remember throwing back a drink and lowering the glass to shout out (voice ratcheting up along the whole of the line, glass thumping down on the final word; I'd suddenly become Sir Lewis Gielgud):

And my poor fool is HANGED?!

For all I know, I may have done the Canterbury prologue as well. Or gone on at untowards, unoccasioned length about Pushkin's black grandfather.

Shortly thereafter we found ourselves on the street bearing aloft the opinion that we could do with food.

Streetlights were shelled in rainbow. Buses heaved their way up out of the fog like mythical, half-remembered beasts and fell back into it. Winds blew in across Lake Pontchartrain, bearing the infant Change in their arms.

When I turned to ask what she'd like, to eat, I meant, *she* came into *my* arms.

Then it got really strange.

At some level I'd known all along, I think, that I was dreaming, but till this point the dreams had clung tenuously enough to reality that I could elect not to question, simply to go along. Now those bonds were forfeited and I was apart, at once *in* the dream and above it looking on.

Had I ridden my bicycle here? Apparently so. And left it outside the bar, where now someone briefly squats down to remove the rear wheel and tucks it beneath his arm as though this were his usual morning baguette, striding away untroubled. I follow him into a nearby art gallery where he's about to hang it around the neck of a bronze ostrich and demand its return. He shrugs and hands it over: no big thing.

But now the bicycle wheel's become a reel of film, and in the passover it's come partially unwound. Thumb jammed at the center, fingers dialing, I start rewinding. Images click against my wrists.

"Guess you must show that to your wife, get her primed and wet, huh?" the bearded man behind the counter says. "Have to tell you: I've handled my share of erotica through here over the years. But *that* damn near made *me* wet."

When I grope for bus fare back out on the street, film tucked beneath my arm the same way he'd carried it, I drop the reel. It hits the pavement and begins smoking. Burns its way through like a cattle brand, making a kind of patterned manhole. I lean over and look. There's a whole subterranean city below. Streets, buildings, cars. Someone walking by down there looks up at me. Our eyes meet.

I awake lying on the floor, eye to eye with Dana, who's just stepped into view above me, naked except for the press pass alligator-clipped to one nipple. Swampy, mothball smell off her body.

"You're ready, aren't you, Lewis?" Definitely I seem to be ready. She lowers herself onto me. "News at six? *Good* news for a change?" Body warm as a bath. Completes itself with my small emendation. Press pass swinging gaily back and forth as she moves above. "Don't forget me, Lew." Moving ever faster as a long moan escapes her. "Whatever happens, don't forget me." She throws her head back in abandon. When she brings it forwards again, her head has become a grinning skull.

"Jesus!"

I started awake—really awake this time—heart pounding, fingernails pushed hard into palms. Probably crescents of bright blood there.

"Bad dreams, my boy?" Standing by the window, from the sound of it.

I heard the tab rip from a beer can, which cinched it. I was getting pretty good at this. Think of men in old movies sitting faithfully before their sonar screens listening to blips.

"My boy, your black ass," I said. "Been reading those damn British novels again, haven't you. Thought you told me you were done with those."

"Yeah. But sometimes what we're done with isn't done with us, you know?"

Time rolled itself millimeters thinner.

"You're a Trollope, Slaughter. A slut, just like Molly Bloom. I ever tell you that?"

"As well you as another."

"Good to see you, Hosie—in a manner of speaking. Thanks for coming."

"How you doing, boy."

"There you go with that boy shit again."

"What can I say? Three generations—"

"—out of slavery. I've read Himes too, remember?"

He pulled the tab on another beer and held it out to me. I reached and found it. Always had his shoulder bag with him those days. Never far from a corner store here in the civilized swamp.

"I most assuredly do remember," Hosie said. "And I'm here to tell you I can groove on that. Know where you're coming from. I hear you."

Once he'd written an entire column on local government in current catchwords and clichés, another time a whole essay in song titles. Hung out in cafés and bus stations and bars just to listen to people talk, then he'd go home afterwards and write it all down. I often wonder what Hosie would have thought if he'd lived into the rap era. He'd have loved hip-hop's special language—*flavor, down on, up for.*

"What time of day you think it is, anyway?" he said. Man never did have any sense of time. Forever ringing doorbells at three in the morning only to say, authentically surprised and apologetic: Hey, I wake you up? I could hear his hand rubbing at the window.

"Everything gray out there. Tops of buildings look the same as sky."

He downed most of the rest of his beer at a gulp and belched magnificently.

"Raining," I said.

And hard, from the sound of it. Water would be rising inch by inch towards midtown porches, trash at curbside all over the city levitating, the Corps of Engineers' clever pumps chugging away at their efforts to push water out of the city and back up to sea level.

"Weather will continue bad, yes. More calamities, death, despair. Not the slightest inclination of a change anywhere. No escape. The weather will not change."

"Henry Miller."

"Very good, sir. Your prize."

He set another beer, cracked open, on the nightstand. Three there now in a perfect row. I'd counted them the way movie cowboys count expended bullets.

"You love them so much, Lew. Literature, the language itself."

"You taught me that, Hosie, a lot of it."

"I did, didn't I? I did." He was quiet a moment. "And I wish like hell they'd never let you down. Everything does, you know, sooner or later."

No answer to that. I didn't try. Rain bucketed down outside. Somewhere a phone rang unanswered; stopped; started up again.

"You've all been taking turns, standing watch," I said.

"Guess we have at that."

"Why?"

He didn't answer, but walked back to the window. I tried to imagine, to summon up within myself, what he was seeing out there. Pinpricks of stars. Diminutive fires of the planet. Everything, as he said, gray. As though we were in some reverse aquarium, a cube of air complete with its own strange creatures, with water all around.

I never found out exactly what it was that had hurt my friend so—something working in him a long time, that finally found purchase. In future years I'd come to recognize similar things scrabbling for footholds within myself. They were already there, of course, even then. Sometimes at night I heard them breathing.

"We care about you, Lew. That's not enough?"

Guess it would have to be.

"I've got a story to write," Hosie said, and left.

DAYS MARCHED IN and out much as Hosie had, appearing unannounced, just as suddenly gone, banners bright or damp. Elsewhere in the world, wars were declared or fought undeclared, sons left home, workers tore open fingers and drove steel rods into their eyes, history smoothed its skirt in place over lap and legs. LaVerne and Hosie brought me tapes: T. S. Eliot, Yeats and Dylan Thomas reading their own work, a five-cassette *Dead Souls*, François Villon.

Two times a day someone appeared, generally an intern or resident, infrequently a nurse, to clean and dress wounds in chest and thigh. Med school professors swept through with students like so many gulping pilot fish in their wake. Meals arrived on covered trays, medications came, phlebotomists entered apologetically, social workers asked about things that were none of their business and went away when I made no response.

LaVerne, Don and Hosie were there frequently, from time to time others: Sam Brown from SeCure Corps, Frankie DeNoux, Bonnie Bitler, Achilles Boudleaux. Doo-Wop even stopped by one morning on his rounds. Things awful slow out there, Captain, he told me.

I listened to the Folkways poetry tape till I'd got it mostly by heart.

One morning LaVerne climbed into bed beside me as the tape played. We'd done this before. Basically the nursing response was threefold. Some thought it was great, no problem. Others insisted it was against hospital policy. (One foot on the floor at all times?) A handful thought it abominable. Nurses in this last category had a penchant for wheeling about and storming back through the door.

"What do you think, Lew? Enough time out? Dinner's been on the table awhile now. Getting pretty cold."

I could smell her perfume, the scented shampoo she'd used, breath sweet with champagne and cheese. Her sweat, that smelled like no one else's. That distant odor she always insisted I imagined, of other men.

"Sooner or later—some things—you have to decide, Lew."

She burrowed closer against me, as into covers on cold mornings.

"I miss you so much, hon."

Some code in their bodies, in our own, stamped and trampled deep, a code we never understand, never learn to read, but respond to.

"And I'm so tired, Lew."

We listened to traffic build outside. How many mornings had we lain like this, LaVerne newly home from work, light filling the world's wide-mouthed jar, all our city's good citizens slipping back into their lives.

Must have been a hard night. LaVerne's breathing slowed, her hands twitched a few times and were still. Within moments she was snoring.

"Love you," I told her.

BOUDLEAUX HAD PICKED up whatever jobs stumbled towards me, handling most of them himself, farming out others to Sam Brown, still with SeCure as consultant but mostly freelancing now.

Once the thought came, I realized it had been at the back of my mind for some time. I tripped the call button.

Moments later a nurse's aide entered. "Yes, Mr. Griffin?"

I held out the card I'd fished from the nightstand.

"Cindy, can you have a look at this, let me know if it's Lee Gardner's card, New York?"

She stepped close to take the card. Her body smelled faintly of garlic and recent sex. It occurred to me that with a peculiar sort of intimacy I knew her voice—and absolutely nothing else about her. Was she twenty, forty? Fat, thin? Plain, pretty? Did she live alone, have a family, kids? Happy to go home at the end of the day, or were nights and days alike just things somehow to be gotten through, endured?

I think that was when (though still I could discern only light and shadow, movement, mass) I knew I was back. Hello world. Miss me?

"Park Avenue. Yes, sir." She read off the number for me. "Would you like me to get it for you, Mr. Griffin?"

About to say I could manage, I thought better. "If you don't mind."

"No sir, I don't mind at all." I sensed her bending beside me for the phone, could see the darkness of her body move against window light. She spoke briefly to the hospital operator then dialed, handing the phone to me. "Ringing."

"Thanks, Cindy. I appreciate it."

"What they all say."

Without visual cues, even the most ordinary social interactions could become problematic. What, exactly, was intended, implied? Confusion must have shown in my face.

"Joshing you, Mr. Griffin. Don't you pay me any mind. I'll check in on you later."

I'd have continued, but just then someone with a clarinet voice said thank you for calling Icarus Books, could she help me.

"Lee Gardner please."

A pause.

"I'm afraid Mr. Gardner is no longer with Icarus Books, sir. Would you care to speak with another editor?"

No.

I see. Well.

Might there be another number at which I could reach him?

Well. Unofficially, of course, you *might* try reaching Mr. Gardner at 827-7342. Thank you for calling Icarus Books.

Alto sax this time, reed gone bad: "Popular Publications."

"Lee Gardner please."

"May I say who's calling?"

I told her.

"Hang on, Mr. Griffin. Lee's probably at lunch. Most everyone is. But I'll give it a shot." She clicked off the line and back on. "Hey. You're in luck." Then her voice sank towards some phonal purgatory, half there, half not: "A Mr. Griffin for you on line two, Lee."

"Yes?"

I didn't often have a phone those days, phones requiring such middle-class imponderables as references and credit, but when I did, I often answered the same way. Or else I'd just pick the thing up and wait.

"How are you, Mr. Gardner?"

"Busy, thank you."

Nothing more forthcoming. Moments ticked like tiny bombs on the wire. I heard his radio move from the Second Brandenburg with screaming pocket trumpets to a jazz station, vintage Miles from the sound of it. Pure jazz stations still existed back then.

"Lew Griffin. We met here in New Orleans. You were looking for one of your writers. Amonas, Amana, something like that."

A brief pause. "Latin."

"Guess it does sound that way, now you mention it."

"You hate Latin much as I did?"

"Never had a chance to. They stopped teaching it the year I hit high school. Stopped teaching all languages that year. No money for it, they claimed. No money, no teachers, no interest. Has to be some advantage in knowing what words like *tenable* really mean, though. Not many do."

"Hell, most don't even have a clue where commas and periods go. Let alone that subjects and verbs should agree."

We fell silent. His radio spun combinations: news, country, rock, something Perry Como-ish. Finally came to rest on what sounded like an adaptation of Karel Capek's *R.U.R.* Back a few years, I listened to programs like that every night. Still remembered one about this doctor treating lepers on an isolated island, trying to atone for wrongs he's done. I'd fallen asleep halfway through and, three in the morning, still half drunk, woke to its conclusion, when a ship comes to retrieve the doctor and he sees in the faces of its crew that *he*'s become a leper.

"Ray Amano," Gardner said.

Behind him on the radio someone said "You've cleared this with the family, I assume," someone else "But he is long dead, in the war."

"Just a moment. Let me jot this down. There. For a project of mine, images of war in popular culture." The radio shut off. Gardner's voice seemed of a sudden eerily loud. "I'm afraid that I don't represent Mr. Amano anymore. Or publish him, for that matter."

When he stopped speaking, static rushed in to fill the quiet.

I waited.

"I do know he's still not been heard from. Kid name of Gilden's editing an edition of *Bury All Towers* for one of those subscriber-only paperback clubs, talking about doing others. He's called me up a couple of times. The Hollywood interest is long gone, of course."

"Can't be *too* long gone. Everybody in such a hurry to let go?"

"It's been almost two months. Burners cool quickly in this business, Mr. Griffin."

. . .

"YOU COULD HAVE told me," I said.

"I *did* tell you, Lew. I told you, the doctors told you, LaVerne told you, Hosie told you. We told you two or three hundred times. Every other way, you were fine, but you just couldn't hold on to time. Time passed right through you, left nothing behind. Doctors say it's the kind of thing that can happen with concussion, severe trauma—or with hypoxia. One of the rounds nicked your femoral artery, Lew, you remember that? You'd bled out pretty bad by the time the paramedics got there."

"Of course I remember." Remembered them telling me about it, anyway.

"Physically, you were well enough to be released some time back."

"But it's only been a few days, a week at the most. I *know* that."

"That's how it seems, Lew. To you—which is precisely the problem."

I'd been Doo-Wopped. Every day was today. I was on Hopi Mean Time.

"Doctors held off discharging you because of that. They say usually the sensorium rights itself, gets back on track without much help from them. Just a matter of time. Or in the case of hypoxia, other parts of the brain learn to take over."

"Or maybe they don't."

"Yeah," Don said. "Maybe."

After a moment I tripped the call bell. Cindy responded.

"I'm leaving, Cindy. Any paperwork has to be signed, they need to get it up here."

"Head nurse'll flip out over this, Mr. Griffin." Her

tone suggested that this was not an altogether unwelcome prospect. "Course, she flips out over almost anything."

"Closet's to your right, about five paces," Don said once Cindy was gone.

I found it and fumbled the door open, one of those push hard and let go affairs. "Anything in there?"

"Ten or twelve empty hangers. Clothes—T-shirts, jeans—folded and stacked on the shelf above, to the left. Socks and underwear right."

"Thanks, Don. I don't suppose there'd be a suitcase, anything like that?"

"Matter of fact there is. Same shelf, far right. I brought one up a couple of days ago. Had a feeling you might be needing it soon."

Within moments clothes were stowed away. Retrieving razor, shaving cream, toothbrush and toothpaste from the phonebooth-size bathroom—not to mention a fifth of Scotch Hosie had smuggled in—I threw them into Don's suitcase and zipped it shut. The suitcase bumped against my leg as I started for the door and walked into the corner of the nightstand. I'd go on collecting bruises for some time.

"Nothing fair about any of it, is there, Don?"

"You ever thought any different?"

At which point Head Nurse pushed imperiously in to begin reciting the litany of reasons I could not, absolutely could *not*, leave.

"Probably shouldn't block the door," Don said. "And I'd stand back if I were you. I know this man."

She ignored him. "You insist on this, I'll be forced to call Security."

Her beeper went off. She ignored that as well.

"Call whomever you want. But you'd be well advised

to call your administrator first, to check on legalities."

Exasperated: "It's five in the *morning*."

"Hey, he'll appreciate it. Let him get an early start."

She swung about and fairly steamed out of port.

Hand against my elbow, Don guided me to the door without seeming to do so.

"What do you think, Lew? Deal with paperwork later?"

"Man after my own heart."

We went down halls smelling of disinfectant, defecation and despair. Stood in a kind of lobby area, voices all a jumble, waiting for the elevator. "Take care, Mr. Griffin," Cindy said as the doors closed. I hadn't known until then that she was there.

"Heading for LaVerne's, I assume," Don said.

"If she'll have me."

Elevator doors whispered open.

"Oh, she'll have you, all right. Fact is, we shut down your apartment, hope that's okay. Your things are in my garage. Didn't think you should be alone—for a while, at least. You okay, Lew?"

"Fine."

"Car's just over there."

His trusty Electra. Don took the suitcase from me, stashed it in the trunk among jugs of water, half a case of oil, jumper cables, medical kit, sheathed shotgun, as I climbed in the passenger door.

He fired up the car and let it idle. Punched in the lighter.

"Always room at my place for you, Lew, things don't work out."

I nodded.

He lit his Winston, which smelled like burning twigs,

and eased the Buick around and down, past the pay booth, onto Prytania, then right towards the river.

"Scenic route, huh?"

He grunted.

"Kind of wasted on me."

"I doubt it. Besides, the air's better over here."

We planed slowly along the curve of river and road. The occasional car passed. This is our new Chevy Occasional, sir. As fine a car as you'll find anywhere. Twice within a single block we bucked across railroad tracks. Then things grew quiet. Don and Lewis in the forests of night. Keeping order here at the edge of civilized space.

"Guess I'll have to find this Dana Esmay person."

A block or two later he responded.

"Yeah. Figured that's what we might be doing. Already penciled it in on my calendar."

Dawn broke about us as I cranked down the window and felt fresh air cascade over my face. Always new beginnings. Something in the backseat, a hat, a plastic cup, went airborne in the sudden tide and flew against a door.

"Whatever works," LaVerne would say years later in similar circumstances. "You wait and see."

So you do.

ears later I wrote a book titled *No One Looks for Eddie Bone*. At the time I was laid up with multiple sprains and a couple of broken bones and I was bored. I'd turned my back on a man who borrowed capital to open an antique shop on Magazine and because the shop wasn't doing well thought he could lay off the payback. I'd been hired as a tutor to help him gain an understanding of basic economics. Knew better than to turn my back, of course, following the brief first lesson. I was thinking that even as the Thirties walnut wardrobe, a real beauty, fell on me.

I'd been a fan of mystery fiction since high school days back in Arkansas, back when I did little else *but* read, three or four books a day sometimes, *Crime and Punishment* lit off the smoldering butt of *Red Harvest*.

Lying there years later, stove up as my old man would have said, one state east and another south, not so very much later, really, though it seemed easily half a lifetime and altogether a different world, I read a paperback Don had brought me, *Such Men Are Dangerous*. It told of a soldier who'd long ago lit out for the territory, away from civilization and all its Aunt Sallys, choosing isolation and a life so simple, so pared down to basic function, as to be virtually ahuman. But the world comes after him there on his tiny island and breaks his solitude, shatters the rigid simplicity that holds him in check.

When I finished the book I didn't go on to another according to habit, but instead turned back to the first and began again. That time I reached the last page thinking maybe this was something *I* could do. It was not a thought I'd had before, and it was occasioned as much as anything else by the simple fact that I didn't want the story to end.

Stories never do end, of course. That's their special grace. Lives end, people die or walk away from you forever, lovers depart in moonlight with paper bags of belongings tucked beneath arms, children disappear. Close *Ulysses* and nothing has ended. Molly's story, Leopold's, Stephen's, Buck Mulligan's—they all go on, alongside yours.

LaVerne brought Big Chief tablets and Bic pens when I asked. What with drugs and pain, I wasn't sleeping much. I started writing one night at eleven or so, *Such Men Are Dangerous* propped (and prop it was, in every sense) against the bedside lamp.

> When I first met Eddie Bone he was wearing a tuxedo jacket shiny as a seal's skin with wear over fatigue pants held up with a rope at his waist. The pants were so big and shapeless it looked like he was wearing a gunnysack. He told me he'd lost his turkey.
>
> I'd heard about Eddie on the street. God knows where he got it, but he had this young turkey, walked around with the thing on a leash.

He'd give it the food he pulled out of trash cans out back of fast-food places and restaurants. Plan was, he was gonna fatten the turkey up and sell it just before Thanksgiving.

Not too long after that, Eddie himself got lost—just disappeared off the street. And no one seemed to care, no one went looking for him. Except me.

"That friend of yours still doing freelance secretarial work?" I asked Verne on her regular visit a couple of mornings later.

"Roberta? I think so. Sure."

Roberta had been Chee-See, Honey Brown and Baby Blue before she'd turned intelligence, determination and substantial savings towards classes at LSUNO and a business degree. In the life, crowding thirty she'd looked sixteen, rare capital. Dividends came in fast, and most of it (over ninety percent, she once told Verne) had gone unspent.

I handed Verne three of the tablets.

"Think she could type this for me?"

"She gets fifty cents a page, Lew."

"So I'll take out a loan."

LaVerne stood reading down through the pages.

"Hey, this is good."

I shrugged and stood slowly, using lots of arm on the dismount, making sure I had my balance before I moved farther. Still hurt like hell. Ribs taped. Muscles that came out of nowhere to settle in like squatters, building fires.

"Get you anything?" I asked LaVerne. "A drink, cup of tea?"

"Beer would be nice."

She carried the tablets over to the swayback couch by the window. I brought her a Jax and, settling alongside, feigned interest in a biography of H. G. Wells, a curious artifact prepared by one of Wells's contemporaries, a die-hard Fabian. Its thesis seemed to be that Wells never put leg in pants, word on paper or penis in vagina without first considering how such activities might be entered by accountants looking after his Socialist ledgers.

When Verne reached out, groping blindly only to find the bottle empty, I brought her another Jax.

Finally she looked up, closing the last tablet, Indian head nodding shut. She sat there a moment.

"It's so sad, Lew."

She tilted the can twice, drank off the last of her fourth beer.

"I knew Christa was going to disappear, but I kept hoping she wouldn't. I knew Lee was never going to find her, and I knew *he* knew, though I guess each of us in our own way kept hoping he might. They're all so *real*, Lew. Even that guy on the uptown streetcar for, what, half a page? I don't know how you do that."

Me either—aside from knowing that I could. It had something to do with capturing voice. All our lives, every day, hour after hour, we're telling ourselves stories, threading events, collisions and recollections on a string to make sense of them, making up the world we live in. Writing's no different, you just do it from inside someone else's head.

"I'll drop it off at Roberta's tonight," LaVerne said.

"Think she'd be willing to bill me?"

"Don't worry about it."

"I don't want you paying for this, Verne."

"She's a friend, Lew."

Verne stood, offering her back. Her dress slid easily over shoulders, head and raised arms. Tufts of hair, scissored short but never shaved, underarm.

Now her head lay in the crook of my shoulder, my hand curled like a snail against her spine. Mozart's bassoon concerto from the radio. Gentle rain outside. Wind moaned at stray corners and windows of the house where daylight was fading.

"Everything slips away, doesn't it Lew."

"If you don't take notice, it does."

"Even if you do."

What could I say?

Let wind and fading light speak for me?

After a moment she raised her head and met my eyes. Her own eyes glistened. The concerto's second movement began. Aching, reluctant. As though once these notes were uttered and released they'd be gone forever, forever irretrievable.

"Can you hold me, Lew? Just hold me?"

"I am holding you, V."

"Then can you just go on? Just for now. So *I* won't slip away."

I could. I did. But I never held her hard enough, or long enough.

To this day I don't know why.

SOME TIME AFTER the shooting, landlocked on Touro's dry continent, sometime in the second month, perhaps, I met the man who loved dead babies.

Those days I spent a lot of time walking, corridors,

hallways, along Prytania just outside, staying close to walls as, still virtually sightless, I paced the limits of my world thinking of caged things. Terrible slowness overtaking haste, as poet Cid Corman put it. Or how Blind Lemon ranged all over Dallas, uptown, Deep Elm, no problem.

One morning, having got off inadvertently on the wrong floor, no one else on the elevator to guide me, I fetched up outside the neonatal intensive care unit.

"Baby Girl Teller's gone."

Not at all certain I was being addressed till a hand touched me lightly and withdrew.

"Baby Girl Teller? Shawna."

"I'm sorry?"

"Last night sometime." Rich aroma of coffee from his breath. "I was here till eight, so it had to be sometime after that. Nurses still in report, I won't know for a while. None of us ever thought she'd last that long, of course. Amazing how hard these kids struggle, isn't it?"

I realized a hand had been extended. Found and took it. Another pause as he noticed my groping.

"Sorry." Faint suggestion of good bourbon beneath the coffee? "Bob Skinner. Have a restaurant over on Adams coming up on ten years now. Can't cook a lick myself, I'd be eating fish sticks and Stouffer's most nights otherwise, but from the first, no reason to it, good people walked in my front door looking for work. They run the place. I have sense enough to get out of the way and let them."

I told him who I was.

"Not from here."

"Not a hell of a lot of us are. Even those of us for whom it's home."

"I know what you mean. I came down twelve years ago for the music. Celebration trip, I told myself: I'd just graduated from City College with a master's in philosophy. What the hell you gonna do with something like that, a degree in philosophy? Might as well train to be a shepherd. When the others went back, I stayed on. My Polish grandmother had left me money smuggled out of Germany. I used it to open the restaurant. Damned thing took off—who'd have ever thought it? You have a son or daughter in there?"

I shook my head. "Just walking by."

"Feeling your way, so to speak." He must have smiled at that. I know I did. "Baby Girl Teller's the third one to die this week. Something they call nec. Dead bowel. IC bleeds get a lot of the others. Kind of like a stroke. That's what took Baby Boy Gutierrez, both the Williams twins, Baby Raincrow. Mario, that's Baby Raincrow, he'd been with us almost three months.

"Top of that, you've got drug babies, chronic hearts, all these syndromes with password names, Down and Tet and the like. Or short rib syndrome, like what Baby Patel had. Diptak, his name was. Always made me think: Tiktok of Oz. Chest wall never develops past what's there at birth. Just growing up kills you. You squeeze yourself to death."

Automatic doors opened. Someone smelling of apples emerged.

"Hey. Sandy."

"Morning, Bob. You ever go home?"

"Sure I do. Break time?"

"You bet."

"Catch as catch can, huh?"

"Better believe it. This day could go down the tubes

fast, any moment. Twenty-seven-week triplets on the board."

"So I heard."

With a discreet *ding*, the elevator sighed open.

"Later, Bob."

"Give the kids a hug for me, Sandy. Rich get over his cold?"

"For now, anyway."

"Woman's a hero," Skinner said as the doors shut. "Her ten-year-old's some kind of musical genius, been giving concerts since she was six, had to have a special cello made for her. Four-year-old's a cystic. Sandy's always been torn between the two of them, what they need. Husband can't handle it at all. Either he's gone completely, out of the picture for months at a time, or he's there bringing her flowers one moment, beating on her the next. Then every day she comes in to worry over *these* kids. Buy you a coffee?"

We descended together to the lobby, where I'd been heading all along. In the cafeteria Skinner pushed my cup across a table sticky with God knows what. We go suddenly into free fall, you could stand on it and be okay.

"Sugar? Cream?"

"I'm fine."

I sat back dipping in and out of nearby conversations. Lawyers with briefcases of restless papers just to our right, cops with crackling radios also nearby, one of them a rookie being talked through a written report, man with a catch in his voice asking How can you do this to me, Thelma, don't you know I'd do anything for you? don't you? as the woman stood and walked away.

"So," Skinner said. "You don't have a kid in NI, what were you doing up there?"

"Told you. I got off on the wrong floor."

"Maybe you were meant to."

Uh-oh, I thought, here it comes. One of those guys who's got it all figured out. Next thing I knew he'd be witnessing to me, wanting to know what church I attended, inviting me to his.

"What about you?" I said.

"Me?"

"Son? daughter? grandchild?"

"No, nothing like that, nothing at all. Not even married—not any longer, anyway. Truth is . . ." He trailed off.

"Name's Lew, right?"

"Right."

"Well, truth is I'm sterile, Lew. Susie, my wife, she had some considerable trouble with that. She fought it, but it finally got on top of her. Can't say I blame her all that much. Up in Minnesota last I heard, living with some student half her age.

"I'm a veteran. Korea—you remember all that? Gave half a lung to the cause of democracy. TB. Things didn't go quite the way they were supposed to. Squirreled out awhile there too, afterward, in the hospital. Sequelae, the docs like to call it. Code for somebody screwed up. So for a few years there I was a frequent flyer as far as hospitals go. Hung out on the wards a lot. ER's, too—*that's* something'll definitely change the way you see the world. Then one day I walked by the nursery. There was this kid in a crib just inside that I'd have sworn was watching me. Even held up his arm that jerky way they do, pointing it at me. So I started going by every few hours, and you know? it was like he was always glad to see me. He'd hold up that shaky arm and smile. Like he'd been waiting. Later I found

out his name was Daniel. Mom was barely fifteen, no pre-
natal care. Came in to have him, then no one ever saw her
again. Nurses named him. One of them finally took him
home with her. Great world, huh?"

The one we have, anyway. Late and soon, getting and
spending, laying waste our powers. All that.

"Boys need a refill?" a waitress asked.

"No thanks." One cup and I already had a buzz on.

"*I'll* have half a cup more if you don't mind, ma'am."

She poured and walked away, shoes slapping at the
floor. House slippers with the backs caved in, no doubt,
latest fashion in American footwear.

"I live four blocks from here," my companion said,
"over by the river, in this tiny little house made out of
cypress and set up on cement blocks. Onion plants growing
from behind the switchplates and electric outlets. Least bit
of wind, windows rattle like dry peas in a pod. Every morning I get up and come see my kids. Come back every afternoon, again at night. Maybe they know I'm here, like
Daniel did. Maybe that way they know *someone* cares, at
least."

I remembered what he'd said about the nurse, Sandy.
"Kind of a hero yourself."

"Nah. I've *seen* heroes."

He was quiet for a while.

"You wanta walk?"

We did. Back out into the lobby, onto Prytania. I
heard the sound of heavy traffic from St. Charles a block
away, smelled garlic from a restaurant across the street. A
delivery truck of some kind pulled in hard, brakes groaning. Snatches of conversation again—

"Man does that to my girl, he ain't safe *no*where!"

"*Hell* of a day."

"He love you, honey?"

—as we walked.

"Back in Korea?" Skinner said.

I nodded. Waited.

"There was a . . . Well, they still called it a powder-house. All the stuff we never used was stored there, all this junk the army kept on sending, God knows why, had contracts for it, I guess. Things we had absolutely no need for, never *would* have a need for, crates of sponges, cases of Sterno. Sterno, for godsake! Pencils in boxes the size of yachts."

I sensed he'd come to a stop beside me.

"You getting tired? Want to head back?"

Reluctantly I nodded. Freedom sounded wonderful in theory, but like some third-world countries I could only handle so much of it. Have to ease my way in.

We walked back through what seemed identical snatches of conversation. As we approached the front entrance Skinner said, "Whenever we got shelled? I'd go to the powderhouse, hide in there till it was over."

THAT YEAR WILL also be remembered as The Year Mother Came to Visit. Red-letter in every way.

"Lewis. Came to help out till you recover," she said when I opened the door.

In my mind's eye I saw her clearly: cheap red dress, plastic shoes, processed hair and her usual clenched expression, face set to keep the world out or herself in, you were never sure which.

Back sometime when I was a teenager, Mother gave

up on life. She walled herself in, began making her way so rigidly through her days that one became indistinguishable from another. Got up the same time every morning, drank the same two cups of coffee, had the same half-lunch and half-dinner, and when she talked, said pretty much the same things over and over again, modular conversation, giving what she said as little thought as she'd given those two cups of morning coffee.

Any change, any variance from routine, could bring oceans of night crashing down on us all.

My old man struggled awhile then gave up himself. He'd come home, have dinner with us, spend the rest of the night up to bedtime out in his workshop. Guess that's some measure of how much he loved her.

Later in my own life I'd realize she was probably schizophrenic. No one in the family ever talked about it, though. And whenever I said anything to sister Francy, she'd just shrug.

All of which is to say that finding Mom there, three hundred miles from home, its failsafes and barricades— she having in addition *flown*, as I soon discovered— astonished me. She might just as well have crossed Ethiopia on camelback.

"You never gave me your new address, Robert."

I was reasonably sure I hadn't given her my old one, either.

"But then I remembered Miss Adams sending me a thank-you card, last year, maybe the one before. Same return address as that sweet note she wrote me when your father died, so I reckoned she must have some kind of roots here."

Stopping suddenly:

"You don't look so good, Robert. Lewis, I mean."

"I'm fine, Ma."

"Sure you don't need to sit down? Have something to eat, maybe? I could make you a cup of coffee."

"I'm okay. Really I am. How'd you find out?"

Met with silence, I pushed against it. "Come on, Mom, it's not a difficult question."

"I'm trying to recall. . . ."

"Bullshit."

After a moment she said: "Guess a boy turns man, goes off to the city, he commences to talking like that."

It was the closest thing to emotion I'd heard in her voice for years.

"I called her, Lew," LaVerne said, stepping in from the kitchen. "I thought she should know. Welcome home, soldier."

"It's okay," I said. "It's okay." I guess to both of them.

"You're hungry, I have a meatloaf back there that just came out of the oven," Verne said. "Potatoes and turnip greens almost done."

You could probably see it in Mother's eyes: Dinner at six in the morning?

"We're not on the same schedule as most folks," I said. "Doesn't mean we're much different from them." But of course it did.

LaVerne stepped closer to Mother, probably touched her lightly.

"I hope you'll join us, Mrs. Griffin."

Ignoring me the same way she ignored that *we*, Mother turned to LaVerne.

"I'd be pleased to, thank you. Nothing I like better in the world than a mess of fresh greens."

They started off together towards the kitchen, me trailing behind. Incredible smells. LaVerne had set the table (I soon discovered) with cloth napkins, wineglasses for water, her best dishes.

LaVerne went to the stove to take things up. Moments later she set down a platter with meatloaf, ceramic bowls of roast potatoes and turnip greens cooked with fatback, plate of sliced onions, mason jar of chow-chow.

I pulled Mom's chair out and she sat. Then I went around to hold LaVerne's.

"Good to see *some* of how we brought you up has stuck," Mother said.

"You just call me Mildred from now on, dear," she told LaVerne.

aving Mother around, I suppose, was no more difficult than learning to swim with cannonballs tied to each extremity. And there *was* something comforting about hearing again (and again and again) the mantras with which I'd grown up.

Why is it you have to do everything the hard way, Lewis?

Stubborn as your father was, I swear. Won't ever be half the man *he* was, though.

Like we always told you, not that you were ever one to listen: Get your education first. Just look at you—don't even have your own place to live.

Mother was someone who never allowed herself anger, never expressed her bottomless disappointment with life. You asked her, everything was always fine. So the pain and despair had to *squeeze* its way out, and it did: everywhere.

It was a long time before I admitted to myself how much I was like her.

We broke the news about my not having an apartment gently (You take the bedroom, we'll sleep out here, perfectly good couch that makes into a bed) and had her installed with the door shut before she had time to object either that she couldn't put us out or that she wasn't about to sleep away this good day the Lord gave us.

Around Mother, somehow the world turned into an endless chain of conjunctions and dependent clauses and qualifiers, just like that last sentence. You learned to keep your feet moving, grab a breath when you could.

Verne in crinkly satin nightgown was asleep instantly beside me. I kept on underwear as a concession to company and lay listening to traffic, thinking about my father's death a few years back, about Hosie's sadness, about my son.

I had an overwhelming desire for music just then. The overture to *Don Giovanni* would have worked. So would have Blind Willie's "Dark Was the Night—Cold Was the Ground."

Seemed all my life, unaccountably, I'd been going from solitary existence to a house full of people and right back to alone. I didn't know then, of course, how adamantly that pattern would continue, how jumbled my life would be, the whole of its length, between private and public.

A branch dipped towards the window, skeletal hand clutching at the life in here.

With a start I realized I'd *seen* it. Watched as the branch bowed towards me. Watched as those fingers reached, scrabbled, and fell away.

I'd *seen* it.

I turned my head to watch Verne's body against the

white wall as she turned from back to side tugging covers along.

I was afraid to close my eyes, afraid it might all go away again.

Our biweekly garbage truck lugged into place out front. I swung legs over and stepped to the window. A lithe young man in khaki overalls leapt from the back, took up our bin and emptied it, then in what seemed a single continuous motion let the bin fall and, whistling to signal the driver to pull out, leapt back onto the truck.

It's possible, given the circumstances, that I may never have seen anything more beautiful.

Pillowlike clouds drifted above the boarded-up mansion opposite. Uniformed children with backpacks, alone and in straggling groups, trod towards school. Bicyclists young and white, old and black, whirred by.

All of it unspeakably lovely.

Look at the same thing day after day, you no longer see it, it goes away. To see again, one way or another *you* have to go away. Then when you come back, for just a while, your eyes work again.

It's a lesson I took to heart, one I'd carry with me the rest of my life.

"THING IS," Don told me, "no one in the department much *cares* who did Eddie Bone. We all figure hey, one less maggot we gotta worry about."

We'd met at a hole-in-the-wall po-boy shop on Magazine, three or four mostly unused and unwashed tables and you didn't want to look too closely at the counter or grill, but the sandwiches were killer. When our order was called,

Don stepped up to a clump of pumped-up kids in hair-nets and bandanas hanging out by the counter thinking about coming on as hard cases. Don just stood there waiting. They looked at his face a moment or two and stepped aside.

"Let me put it this other way. Shrimp, right?" He handed mine across. Shreds of lettuce hanging out like Spanish moss off trees in Audubon Park. "They've got means, since the case is still officially open. And they've got opportunity. What they don't have is motivation."

He bit into his roast-beef po-boy. Gravy squirted onto paper plate, table, chin, shirt, tie.

"There's really no investigation under way, then."

"The matter's 'not being actively pursued' according to department jargon, right. We get fifteen, twenty homicides a month, Lew, more during summer months. When all our ducks line up—when the city's not cutting back again, none of our people get shot or sick, none of them has family problems or turns out a drunk—we've got six detectives to the shift."

Don finished off his sandwich and drank the last of his iced tea.

"Hey, you want a beer?"

"Ever know me not to?"

I finished my own sandwich as Don went back to the counter. No hesitation this time. The kids saw him get up and stepped away.

We took our beers outside. There were a couple of picnic benches each side of the street corner, but like the tables inside they rarely saw use. Most people just came up and ordered through the window, takeaway. Don and I claimed the table furthest off Magazine. Sat there watching the noontime rush. Not much of a rush compared to other major cities, but it's ours.

"You get much sleep?" Don said, reminding me that he'd dropped me off at LaVerne's only a few short hours ago.

I shook my head.

"Me either. Hard to remember when I did. Three in the morning I'm laying there trying to figure out if it's because of the alcohol I'm not sleeping, or if alcohol's the only reason I catch any sleep at all."

Bolted into cement, our table sat beneath a tree that birds of every sort seemed particularly to favor—perhaps for its pungent, oily smell? Don leaned on one ham to wipe pasty greenish-white birdshit off the seat of his pants. The shop provided rolls of paper towels instead of napkins. This being one of Don's regular stops, he'd ripped off several panels when he picked up the beers.

"Verne okay?"

I nodded.

"Good. You tell her I said hello."

I nodded, and we had a few more sips of Jax.

"That mother of yours is a piece of work, Lew."

"She is that."

"She just plain hate white folks or what?"

Though God knows the last thing I wanted to do was make excuses for her, I found myself saying, "No, not at all. More like white people's lives just don't have anything to do with the one *she* leads." I stopped, shaking my head. "It's complicated, Don." Probably there was no way I could ever explain it to him. "Where she's from, it's all pretty clear, on both sides."

"You're from there, too."

"Not far enough."

Neither of us spoke for a while.

"Wife keeps asking me about you, Lew. What do you think you owe that black man? she says. My life, I tell her.

"I got home this morning, she started up again. You already *paid* that debt. Kids and I hardly see you, when we do you're so tired it's all you can do just to eat and fall in bed. Now here you've stayed up half the night driving this black man around.

"He's my friend, I told her. Walked back out the door and went to work."

"That's one way of ending an argument."

Don laughed. "Sometimes it's the only way. You want another beer, Lew?"

"Not really."

Traffic began easing off. Couple of hours later there'd be a second tide as schools let out, another starting about four-thirty.

"Yeah. Me either, I guess."

"Any chance you and Josie might come to dinner some night, Don? Verne makes a kickass gumbo. One bite of her court bouillon, you'll be grinning like a catfish and looking for mud to swim in."

Moments went by. Don let out a long breath. "I don't think Josie'd be able to do that, Lew. Sorry. Maybe someday."

"I understand."

Ancient time, once battles were over, scavengers appeared on battlefields, moving from body to body, retrieving what they could. All of us do the same with our pasts, our personal histories and relationships. Everything is salvage.

I drained my beer and stood.

"On the hoof as usual?" Don said.

I nodded.

"If you don't want a ride, then—"

I didn't.

"—mind if I walk along?"

We went up Magazine, past a block of doubles being remodeled, windowless, painters inside, stacks of new lumber and piles of old bricks in the yard, towards St. Charles. A scrawny, big-bellied cat followed us partway.

"Word is, there's someone who *does* care," Walsh said. "About Eddie Bone."

We'd stopped at a corner.

"Ever hear of Joe Montagna?"

"Joey the Mountain," I said. "Sure. He have some place in this?"

The light changed and we started across. Eyes tracked us from within an old Ford truck with welded fenders, a new Datsun, a Lincoln whose expanse of flat hood put one in mind of aircraft carriers.

"Who knows? He's been asking questions, though. About you, about the mystery woman."

"Not Eddie Bone."

After a moment Don shook his head. "Not directly."

"And where's he been asking all this?"

"Around. Popping up here and there. Pretty much on the quiet, too. Patrol tells me his home roost's a back table at Danny Boy's, lounge down by—"

"I know where it is."

"Sure you do." Don stopped walking all at once, no warning. "Enough of this exercise shit. I'm heading back for the car while I still have a chance of getting there. Guess you also know Joey's a foot soldier for Jimmie Marconi, huh."

"Word was, he retired."

"Sure he did. And snakes don't bite, they just kiss you real hard."

"Guess I better ask him about that when I see him, how's his retirement going."

"What you better do is be fucking careful."

He started to turn away.

"You need help, anything I can do, you let me know."

"Thanks, Don."

He grunted and trudged towards his car, six or eight blocks back.

BEAR IN MIND that much of what I'm telling you here is reconstructed, patched together, shored up. Like many reconstructions, beneath the surface it bears a problematic resemblance to the model.

For most of a year my life was a kind of Morse code: dots of periods and ellipses, dashes, white space. I'd think I remembered some sequence of events, then, looking back, hours later, a day, a week, I'd be unable to retrieve it, connections were lost. Sidewalks abutted bare brick walls. I'd step off the last stair of LaVerne's midtown apartment onto the levee downtown, Esplanade or Jackson Avenue, the concrete rim of Lake Pontchartrain. Faces changed or vanished before me as I went on speaking the same conversation: like some ultimate, endless compound word that finally managed to include everything.

Holes in my life.

Much of that year then, for me, is gone. History never

so much chronicles the continuities of daily life as it signals the pits opening beneath, upheavals of earth around—the ways in which that life was interrupted. My life became history that year.

Don's filled in part of how Lew spent his vacation, LaVerne much of the rest. After the first dozen or fifteen times they talked to me about it and I promptly forgot what they said, I started taking notes, researching my own biography. Those chinks remaining (and they're considerable) I've filled as best I can with imagination's caulking, till I no longer know what portion of this narrative is actual memory, what part oral history, what part imagination.

Back then not many black men walked into Danny Boy's. Those who did, they'd just humped several dozen cases of beer and booze from delivery truck to back room and were coming round front to have invoices signed. When he was feeling charitable the barkeep would draw off a beer for them while he looked over the invoices.

My face and general size were all that registered with today's barkeep at first glance. He was fiftyish, hair like a well-used steel wool pad, black T-shirt faded to purple. The image on the shirt had faded too, like good intentions or hopeful prospects. He'd grabbed a glass and turned to fill it from the tap before it occurred to him there hadn't *been* any deliveries.

He looked closer at my black suit, blue shirt and tie. Godzilla might just as well have come into his bar and primly ordered a daiquiri.

By then the beer glass was half full. He let go of the tap's paddlelike handle. Dumped the beer and ditched the glass. It bobbed in a sinkful of others.

"Do something for you, boy?"

Stepping up to the bar, I didn't respond. Our faces were two feet apart. His eyes slid sideways, right, left. What the hell: he was on his own ground here. Safe.

Four elderly men sat over a game of dominoes at a nearby table. Three others off to my right threw darts at a much-abused board. No one at the back booth.

"Looking for Joe Montagna," I said.

"Never heard of him."

I let several moments go by. Sand through fingers. These are the days of our lives.

"Tell you what. You take some time, think about it, much time as you need. I'll sit here quietly with a beer while you do. Whatever you started drawing up before's fine."

The barkeep crossed his arms atop a small, hard mound of belly.

"I ain't serving you, boy, you hear? Ain't about to. Best advice I have for you is to go right back out that door."

Domino and dart games had stopped.

"I'd like that beer now, sir, if you don't mind." I held out a hand, fingers spread. "What can we do? It's the law."

He shrugged and moved closer to the bar. "Hey. You're right." He reached for a glass with his left hand, the one I was supposed to follow, while his right hand snaked beneath the bar.

Baseball bat? Length of pipe wrapped in tape? Handgun?

I grabbed the front of his T-shirt and hauled him across. Maybe closer up I'd be able to make out what that faded image was. Momentarily he looked like one of those figurehead mermaids from the prow of a ship. His T-shirt collar began to rip.

"What's the *second* best advice you have for me?"

I heard a rush of air and a sharp whistle close by my right ear as a dart flew past and buried itself behind the bar square between a bottle of Dewar's and one of B&B crawling with gnat-size insects.

I looked around. Players had parted right and left to reveal the thrower, three darts intertwined in left-hand fingers, another in his right ready to go.

"Step away," he said.

I'd kept my hold on the barkeep. Now I dragged him the rest of the way across the bar, scattering glasses, half-filled ashtrays, stacks of napkins and cheap coasters, salt and pepper shakers. Hand at belt and collar, I swung him around in front of me.

Some way off, a toilet flushed. Then, as a door behind a baffle opened, the barest flare of light near the back wall. Light's absence became a dark figure.

No one moved—except that dark figure.

"Step down, gentlemen," he said, a sixtyish, stocky man in charcoal-gray Italian suit, ice-blue Quiana shirt, dark tie, moving unhurriedly towards us.

"Griffin, isn't it? How about a beer? First you'll have to turn loose of old Shank there, though," which I did.

"Two cold ones."

The barkeep shook his newly manumitted head.

"Ain't serving him, Mr. Montagna. Don't matter who tells me I got to."

Joey raised his head maybe a quarter-inch. The knot on his tie didn't even move.

"In my booth, please."

We sat waiting, watching one another across a floe of pale Formica. Shank brought the beers. Joey thanked him.

"Heard some about you, Griffin."

I waited.

"Most all I hear is good—long as a man don't find himself crossed with you."

I raised my glass in a toast. "You've been asking questions."

He lifted his own in acknowledgement, drained it in a single draw.

"You wanted to know about me, you could have gone to your own people. Jimmie Marconi, for instance."

"What makes you think I haven't?"

With no signal I caught, Shank brought fresh beers.

"Jimmie said hands off. Now that was surprise enough, Jimmie not being one to put his marker in. He takes care of his business, leaves the rest of us alone to do ours, everything runs smooth that way. What floored me was this other thing he said. You tell Lewis to come see me, he said, when it's convenient. *When it's convenient.* Forty years I worked at Jimmie's side and I never once heard him say that before, not to no one."

eonardo's was a time capsule they forgot to bury. The restaurant had been there forever; nothing about it ever changed. Same flocked red wallpaper, same portraits of owners hung high on the walls, same ancient black man sitting on a stool by the side entrance rocking and nodding. Inside, there were no windows, and waitresses in beehive hair went about the same business they'd gone about for forty years or more. The menu ran to heavy Italian, with a handful of New Orleans specialties, barbecued shrimp, roast-beef and oyster po-boys, bread pudding, thrown in for good measure. Once you'd snapped off the heads and spurted juice across the silly apron they insisted you wear, the barbecued shrimp finally didn't taste much different from the lasagna. But no one in his right mind came to Leonardo's for the food.

I was never sure why they did come. Maybe this was where the folks used to bring them on special occasions when they were kids or where, he in scratchy wool suit, pajamas underneath, and the family Dodge with its green visored windshield, she in long pleated skirt and flats, they'd had their first almost-grown-up date. Perhaps they all simply took comfort from the fact that in here, no matter what cataclysms took place outside, nothing changed.

Jimmie Marconi came because he'd always come here. His old man had come here and *his* old man before him. Places like New York, Boston, you'd have a regular neighborhood, do business from a booth in the bar on the corner or out of a family restaurant with checkered tablecloths, candles and pots of good, thick marinara reeking of garlic and fresh basil bubbling in the kitchen. That's the way things worked. People wanted to find you—request a favor, ask for justice, tell you their daughter'd got knocked up by some guy refused to do the right thing—they knew where to come. Here it was different. No neighborhood, families spread out all through the city, across the river, out by Kenner and Jefferson. But when they needed you, they still knew where to come.

"You don't want to do this, boy," the ancient black man told me as I stood with one foot on the cement step up to Leonardo's.

"Probably right," I said, entering as he went back to rocking and nodding.

I pushed my way like an icebreaker past the front desk, through baffles of small rooms and beehived waitresses, around the shoal of a chattering, bantamweight maître d' in double-breasted suit, to the main dining room.

Faces turned to watch me. Conversations stopped.

A guy whose neck put me in mind of bulls sat over an espresso at a table near the door. Sucking on a lemon slice, he lumbered to his feet as I came in. So did his counterpart, all wire and nerve endings, at a rear table.

Jimmie's head rose, too. He regarded me for a moment, two, three, nothing showing in his face. Then his hand came up an inch or two. The bookends sat down.

I did the same, across from Jimmie, who tucked back into his plate of cannelloni and, finishing that, pulled close a bowl of cantaloupe with shaved prosciutto.

"You eaten yet?"

I shook my head.

"Mama Bella'd be happy to fix you up something special."

"Mama's other patrons might not appreciate that, sir."

Jimmie nodded and ate his melon slowly, pushing the bowl away when he was done. Then he spoke to the room:

"Closing up in here now, folks. Any of you have food coming, they'll bring it to you out front. Please keep your wallets in your pockets, though; tonight your money's no good. Please have a complimentary drink, too, while waiting—and please come back."

We watched as customers slid from booths and stood, tugging at polyester sport coats, cotton skirts and silk dresses before shuffling out.

"You too," he told his bookends when the citizens were gone.

They didn't like it—eyes flashing *You know you can't trust these people*—but they left.

"Have a coffee with me at least?"

"Sure."

Busboys in yellow vests and black pants came through a doorway at the back of the room to retrieve dishes.

"Sister doing okay, Joseph?" Jimmie asked one of them.

"Yessir. Thank you, sir."

"Heading for college this fall, I understand," Jimmie said to the other, who nodded. "You know you got a job here anytime you need it, right? Summers, holidays. Anytime."

They took the dishes away. Moments later the one whose sister was doing okay returned with two espressos.

"Good health," Jimmie said.

I nodded. One healthy sip and my coffee was gone. Jimmie held the saucer in his left hand, up close to his face, working the cup with his right. Something axlike about that face. Sharp nose, narrow features. Eyes like wedges.

"Don't know as how I ever sat across the table from a black man before."

No response called for—none I'd care to give, at any rate.

Jimmie's hand fluttered up. No one seemed to be watching, but fresh coffees materialized.

"We've known each other now what? four, five years? I try to keep track of you. What it looks like to me is, you have trouble enough keeping track of yourself."

What could I say?

"That's what we're here for, Griffin. To bear witness, to take notice. Ever doubt that, you just look into a child's eyes."

"Your man, Joey the Mountain. He's been asking about me."

"Not anymore he ain't."

"And about the woman I was with the night I got shot."

Jimmie sipped at his coffee.

"You doing okay, right? From the shooting. You recovered."

I nodded.

"That's good." Jimmie threw back the last spoonful or so of his espresso. "Never could get where I was able to care much for this stuff, but I keep trying. What I want is a drink. You want a drink?"

I didn't catch any signal, but the maître d' materialized at our table.

"Single-malt Scotch suit you?" Jimmie said.

"Always has."

"Two doubles, Marcel."

They were there in a blink. I picked up mine and looked through it, remembering how she'd done that very thing in the dive down on Dryades. I swirled the first taste, oily, deep, abiding, over the back of my tongue. Life was good.

"What we hear is, Eddie Bone called you that night."

"He did. Said I should catch him at the club later on."

"He didn't say what he wanted."

"No."

"He ever call you like that before?"

"No again."

Jimmie wet the tip of his tongue with Scotch. He put the glass down before him on the table and sat looking at it.

"We want the woman," he said.

"Why?"

"Not something you ask."

Okay. I had another taste. "What about the shooter?"

Marconi shrugged. "He turns up, we want to talk to him. Where you from?"

I told him.

"You got snapping turtles up there, right? Big fuckers

that look like rocks, move just about as fast. And once they bite down—it don't matter what on, a stick, your hand—they don't let go till it thunders. I figure you're like those turtles, get your beak onto something, you don't let go. No way you're gonna hold off looking for this woman."

The maître d' brought new glasses of single malt. Crystal. Strictly Sunday best: I don't think regular folks in regular clothes and regular lives got them. We sat quietly.

"Maybe this time I help *you*," Jimmie said after a while.

"Sounds to me like any help rendered here, it would be mutual."

"So we help one another, then."

He slid a four-by-six photo across the table. Dana Esmay looked out at me.

"You understand how it is. Our people walk in down there, everything stops. They start asking questions, suddenly everybody's deaf and halfway out the door. You, it's different. You know the scene, people know you. Fifty a day plus expenses sound about right?"

"Couple of conditions. I report only to you—"

"No problem."

"—and I say it's over, whatever the reason, it's over. No questions asked."

"Don't see why not."

I polished off my Scotch. When I was a kid, Mom made pitchers of Kool-Aid, poured it into bright-colored spun-aluminum glasses, green, gold, silver, blue. Other kids gulped theirs down in an instant. My own sat for half an hour as I sipped and savored. They never understood how I could do that.

"Anything you need, information, money, names,

you only have to call. My private number's on the back of the photo."

"Thanks. Better get to work, huh?"

I was almost to the door when he spoke.

"Appreciate what you did for my daughter, Griffin."

The etiquette of these things dictated that I not mention it until he did; now I was free to ask.

"She okay, then? Still at home?"

"Nah. Was for a while. Says much as she loves me she can't be around me. Too much baggage's the way she puts it. Too much stuff cluttering up the shelves. Last I heard from her she's living with this older guy up in Jackson. Both of them got custom Harleys, his jet-black, hers pink, make their living, such as it is, hauling all this shit in a trailer—old army equipment, dolls, iron cookware—between flea markets. Talk about too much crap cluttering up the shelves. So how long's *that* gonna last? I don't see her much, or hear from her. Not directly. But at least I know she's alive. Thanks for coming in, Griffin."

I had to wonder when was the last time Jimmie Marconi thanked someone.

TWO GUYS HAD her back in the kitchen. They'd bent her forward over the table and kicked her legs apart and one of them, a congenital lowlife named Duke Heslep, was holding her there, hands pushed down on her shoulders, while the other one bucked in and out and whenever she made a sound pulled at the hair he'd wrapped in one fist.

Heslep's who I was looking for. Week before, when his trial date on an assault charge rolled up, he'd failed to show. Holding Heslep's bond, Frankie DeNoux wound up forfeiting, not the sort of story's end Frankie much cared for. So he commissioned a sequel, suggesting that I locate Mr. Heslep and remind him of his duty as a citizen.

Half a day of asking questions and making myself a general pain in the ass led me to an abandoned apartment house in the weblike tangle of streets just uptown of Lee Circle and riverside of St. Charles. The door stood open— off its hinges, in fact, and leaning against the wall. Inside there seemed to be two categories of bodies: those caught up in some contemporary version of the tarantella, and those stoned or otherwise semicomatose on couchs, stained mattresses and floor.

Largely unnoticed, I walked through the former and stepped over and around the latter to another open doorway rear left.

"*Sweet* young stuff, Duke. You gonna want some once I'm done."

The one on the joyride had his back to me. Duke stared in fascination at the wavelike motion of the girl's buttocks when his friend drove into her. I was there beside them before they knew it.

"Who the fuck—" Duke began.

I grabbed his hair and slammed his face against the table, putting an end to his curiosity.

The other guy fell out of the girl as he stepped towards me. He landed a quick, hard jab with his left as his right came around for a hook—a great punch, but it quickly lost force since I now had a death grip on his privates. I hung on and squeezed. Hoped I was tight enough for him.

When finally it penetrated that things had changed, the girl, without moving any other portion of her anatomy, turned her head, face blank, pupils black buttons. Her eyes went from the hand I had clamped on the guy's privates to the one still pressing Duke's face against the table, blood from his broken nose pooling beneath. Then she looked at me.

"What do *you* like?"

Using his privates like the handle of a shotput, I threw Humper against the wall. He slid down it into a huddle, hugging himself and retching. Then I pulled Duke upright, hand still wrapped in his hair, and told him he was coming with me. Blood glopped onto his shirt when he nodded.

I marched him out through bodies and down the stairs. His eyes darted about looking halfheartedly for help he was not going to get. Only when we were outside did I realize the girl had followed us.

She'd come around enough to look confused by then, a definite improvement over the blankness I'd seen before. She was still pretty vague, though, and still naked, which even in New Orleans could be a problem.

"Take your clothes off," I told Heslep.

We must have been quite the sight walking up Felicity to where I'd left the car, this white guy in underwear shirt and Jockey shorts, black socks and shoes, bleeding all over himself, spaced-out young woman holding up clownsize pants with both hands as alternately she bounced off walls and staggered off the curb into the street, big buck nigger in black suit bringing up the rear.

I didn't want to think about what would happen if a police car cruised by. Mostly, unless there was a specific call, they stayed out of this part of town.

"And that was Marconi's daughter?" Verne said. "Anyone want more?"

I accepted the platter of ham and sweet potatoes as Mother said "No thank you, dear."

"Yeah. I didn't know it then, or for a long time, really. Figured she was just another messed-up kid. Lots of them around those days. I called Frankie DeNoux to meet me downtown, dropped Heslep off at his new rent-free accommodations, then asked the girl if she had someplace, a home, a friend's place, where she could go. She looked up at me with these strange, hollow eyes.

"Sure," she said, and started away. I watched her turn the corner.

Moments later, she was back. "I don't," she said. "Not really."

"Wait, let me guess. You took her home."

I nodded.

"Lew picks up strays," Verne said to my mother. "Can't seem to help himself."

"It was just for a few days. Once I got her settled in, she was out like a light. I didn't do much better myself, woke up fully dressed with my head on the kitchen table. I put her in touch with a friend of Don's who ran a halfway house. Went to see her a couple of times while she was there. Mostly we'd sit and watch TV together. Then after she got out she started coming by my apartment once or twice a week. Never said much about what she was doing, where she was living."

"And you didn't ask, of course."

People want to tell me something, I listen. What they don't want to tell me is their business, I figure they have reasons.

"What she did talk about a lot then was stuff she was reading, all these thoughts clambering about in her head.

One week she'd show up having just read Hesse, or *The Seven-Storey Mountain*, and that's where everything would begin and end, that was the whole world. Maybe life wasn't about possessions, about personal gain or power, she'd tell me, maybe what was important was this struggle, trying to understand yourself and others even when you knew you never could. Or she might talk about communities, what they were, how important it was to become part of one, to turn away from what she called the lure of your own reflection in the mirror."

"I can't remember being that young anymore, Lew. I know I was, all those grand thoughts running through me, but I can't remember it, can you?"

"Some days, a few good days, I'm *still* that young."

Verne nodded. "Let me get coffee started."

She came back with the sugar bowl and a quart carton of Schwegmann milk. "Ready in a minute."

"Her name was Mary Catherine, but she went by Cathy. Didn't take me long to catch on to how smart she was, and I asked if she'd thought about college. '*You* didn't go to college,' she said, "and you know everything.' What I knew, I told her, I'd managed to learn the hard way, assbackwards and stubborn like I did most things, reading books the way ore companies strip-mine mountains, taking what I could of the best stuff and leaving the rest in ruin, and I wasn't about to recommend that for anyone else.

" 'It can get expensive,' I told her, 'but there are all kinds of scholarships and loans available.'

"I remember her looking up at me and saying, 'Oh, that wouldn't be a problem.'

"Month or so later she tells me she's been accepted up

at LSU. She'll come visit on holidays, she says, and she does, the first couple, but then she stops. Not that I was surprised. Never expected anything else."

Verne went to the kitchen, returning with coffeepot and hotpad. Cups were already set out on the table. She poured.

"You still didn't know who she was?"

"Not a clue. I must have changed living quarters a couple of times in the next few months, I was doing that a lot then—"

"At least you *had* a place," Mother said.

LaVerne's eyes met mine. She shook her head gently.

"Then one day I'm coming home, around the big house and through unruly hedges—I was supposed to cut them, as part of my rent, but never got around to it—to the little one where I live out behind, and someone's waiting by my door, looks like he might juggle tractors to stay in shape.

" 'Do something for you?' I ask.

" 'Nope.'

"I have the keys in my fist, sticking out between fingers.

" 'You Griffin?'

"Yeah.

" 'Jimmie Marconi says he appreciates what you did for his kid.'

"I don't know this Marconi *or* his kid, I tell the guy.

" 'Sure you do. Mary Catherine.' His eyes remind me of Cathy's back when I first saw her. Flat, blank, affectless.

" 'She's okay, then?'

"He shrugs. 'How okay's someone like that ever get?

You askin' me if she's straight, yeah, she's straight. For now.'

" 'Look, it's hot out here. You want a beer?'

" 'Mr. Marconi told me I should find you and tell you this, so I did. Now you got his message. No way I'm goin' in your house, sit down with you.'

" 'Okay,' I said after a moment.

" 'Mr. Marconi says you ever need a favor, anything he can do for you, come see him.'

" 'Thank him for me. But what I did had nothing to do with him.'

" 'In Mr. Marconi's world, *everything* has to do with him.' And tipping one finger to his hat, he waded away into the hedges, merry mystery to all and to all a good night."

I was sipping brandy by this time. Mother peered pointedly at my snifter each time I swirled or lifted it.

"Sounds like you sure got to know yourself some fine folk here in the city," she said.

"I know who I have to know."

Verne touched her wrist softly. "Lew's good at what he does, Mildred." Pressure remained a moment. Then to me: "What's next?"

"What else? I hit the streets."

"Carrying as cargo your photo of the mystery lady, hoping some sailor, in some port somewhere, may have seen and remember her."

"Doesn't sound like much to go on, does it, once you strip it down like that."

"Maybe you could lay off some of the bet, Lew. You know someone who's all *over* this city every day, uptown, downtown, sideways and in between. Finding out what the regulars are up to, finding out who's new in town, where they came from, why they're here."

"Doo-Wop."

Verne nodded. "More coffee, Mildred?"

"No thank you, dear. Dinner was fine as always, but I think I'll be off to bed now. You-all here in the city eat considerable later than I'm accustomed to. And try as I might, I can't make much sense out of this getting to bed at one or two in the morning some days, sleeping your whole way through others."

"Rest well, Mildred."

Verne freshened my brandy and poured one for herself. We sat for a while in silence. She got up and kicked off her shoes, put on *Cosi Fan Tutti*, reached under her shirt to pull off her bra (which she hung on a doorknob) and stretched out beside me on the couch. We listened to the sounds of traffic, to the call-and-response of people walking by outside. Mozart's music broke over us like water in a brook.

"I can help too, Lew. I'm out there every night. Lot of us are. Your woman's still in town, chances are good that sooner or later one of us, one way or another, could come across her."

"I ever tell you how wonderful you are?"

"I'm not sure. I'll check my notes tomorrow. Right now I don't want to move."

"Not working tonight, then?"

"I called a while back. Victoria says she'll cover for me."

"Your regulars won't mind?"

"They all like Vick. Everybody does."

"Want another brandy? Coffee?"

She shook her head. Moments went by. Body warm and still beside me. Music washing over us.

"I like this, Verne. I like what my life's become with you in it. I like what *I've* become."

She raised herself on elbows so that we were face-to-face. "You should, Mr. Griffin," she said. "You most definitely should."

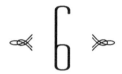

My thoughts kept circling back to a couple of things
those days. Vietnam was scarcely over, all that
ungodly mess in Central and South America just
beginning to surface.

The first was a passage from (I think) *Man's Fate*, describing how someone has withdrawn from the world; how
still, as he reaches for his book, for his pipe and tobacco
tin, his arm enters—moves through—that world around
him.

Second was something Bob Dylan said about peace,
that periodically everybody had to stop to reload and while
they were reloading, those few moments, *that* was peace.

Ten o'clock the next evening as I walked into Soft
Machine deep in the Quarter, those notions were stomp-
ing through my mind in heavy boots again. Soft Machine
was the only bar in town back then devoted to new jazz. A
dozen patrons comprised a rush and two or three was the
usual run, while up the street, at Preservation Hall, people
stood in line for hours to sit on folding chairs as at a

graveside and hear the millionth wooden reprise of "When the Saints Go Marchin' In." I'm all for tradition, God knows, but tradition doesn't just *stop* at some arbitrary signpost; it's not some fossil, a scorpion in amber; it's on-going. That's the whole point.

"There he is, ladies and gentlemen," Bo said. "How's it going, Lew? Been a while."

His first year in high school, Bo'd been principal trombonist, won a fistful of blue ribbons playing stuff like "Flight of the Bumblebee" and "Carnival of Venice." Then his band director, a Canadian named Robert Cinq-Mars who played mean clarinet and wrote his own music, introduced him to jazz. Next thing you know, Bo's looking up old players, hanging out with them whenever he can at jazz funerals, house parties, recording sessions, bars. He'd had a band himself awhile, a damned good one. Then he heard Dolphy and Parker and his life changed again. He knew he couldn't play like that, no way, and he put his trombone down for good, but he couldn't leave the music alone.

"What can I say, Bo? Don't get out much anymore."

"I had someone like LaVerne at home, I wouldn't get out at all. Speaking of which." He shoved a napkin across the bar, number scrawled on it. "She says call her."

"How long ago?"

"I don't know. Hour maybe."

"You seen Doo-Wop?"

"Not for a day or so. Couple of conventions down-town, I figure he's staying busy."

The skinniest young black man I'd ever seen—he looked like an ambulatory twig—climbed onstage. *Stage* was definitely a euphemism for this inch-high flat of rough lumber we'd have used back home to stack feed bags. He plucked a soprano sax out from behind a chair. Held it vertical in his lap as he disengaged the reed from the mouthpiece and put it in his mouth to soak. Another musician took his seat behind the piano. He hit several chords, ran scales and arpeggios off higher intervals of them, pawed at a few jagged, Monklike phrases, then sat with hands in lap waiting.

"Stick around. These guys are unbelievable. I don't know *where* it all comes from," Bo said. "Drink?"

"When'd you last make coffee?"

"What's today?" He poured a cup and pushed it towards me on the bar. "Just kidding. Hey, you're still in New Orleans. I don't keep good coffee, they take away my license, deport me to Algiers, Chalmette. Rip the towel off my shoulder." He angled one long finger towards the napkin. "Phone's still where it was, you get ready."

I turned around on the stool, turned back.

"Seems to be in use."

"Nah. That's just Crazy Jane. Comes in here every night, has a few drinks, spends the next hour or so having imaginary conversations with old lovers."

Grasping the receiver in a death grip at least a foot from her head and shouting into it, Crazy Jane gave way without comment when I tapped on the booth. She replaced the receiver as though setting down an eggshell. I dialed the number on the napkin. The phone rang twice.

"LaVerne there?" Never knew who might be at the other end of one of LaVerne's numbers.

"Who's this?"

"This is the guy who's calling for LaVerne."

"Yeah? Sounds like just another turkey to me."

"You took your head out of your ass, you might hear better."

"You got a definite point there."

He backed the phone off a few inches and shouted: "Hey, O'Neil! Walsh up there? Well, he's for damn sure around here *somewhere*. Yeah you do that." Moments passed. "Griffin's on the line, boss." A staccato exchange of words. "Who else's it gonna be, mouth like that? Hey, always a pleasure talking to you, Griffin." He handed the phone over.

"Lew."

"I got a message from LaVerne to call her at this number. She okay?"

"She's fine. Took her statement myself and sent her home in a black and white almost an hour ago. I asked her to call you."

Crazy Jane stood outside the booth patiently waiting. When I smiled, she smiled back, then ducked her head shyly like a schoolgirl.

"Verne said she was trying to help you find this Esmay woman, from the shooting. So she talked it up on the street— 'just like setting out trot lines back home,' she said. Got her first bite around dinnertime, second one not long after. Hell of a lot better than *we* ever did, or were gonna do. 'Lew says you always hang back,' she told me, 'see what the traffic looks like, give the landscape a chance to become familiar.' She had a couple of coffees at the café on the corner and kept her eyes open, came up here and walked into this."

THIS WAS THE messy anteroom of an apartment in a cul-de-sac off Jane Street.

Built in 1890 as a private home, the building persisted as such, various families moving in and out like hermit crabs, until 1954, at which time it came onto its first abandonment. The Sixties saw its irregular stories and multiple courtyards reincarnated as luxury apartments; late in the decade, following extensive consultations with lawyers, the building's new owners gave it over to use as an orphanage. Shortly thereafter began its second long decline.

These days, though a successful temp agency occupied its bottom floor, the rest remained an urban ghost town. Periodically movies were shot in those rambling uppers: crews would sweep in with brooms, paint and props, drape and hammer and arrange it all to look how they needed it, then disappear, leaving behind new habitats for the wild cats who lived there.

Don showed up to ransom me from the twenty-year-old pillar-of-salt sentinel stationed street level, front door. We climbed narrow, listing stairs gone to rot and splinters, ducked through a sagging walkway.

Dana Esmay lay slumped just inside the entrance to apartment 3-B. A divider wall opened at either end into living room and kitchen areas. Green flocked wallpaper had been mostly torn away; what remained looked like healthy patches of mold. A dozen or so hats and caps hung from nails pounded into the wall.

"We figure she was squatting here," Don said.

"Someone was."

"Evidence of the same in a couple of other apartments on the floor below. Power came from an extension cord, one of those heavy-duty orange ones. It's plugged into an external outlet on the patio downstairs."

I lifted a hat off one of the nails, checked its size, held it close above what was left of her head.

"Look like a fit to you?"

Don nodded. "I see your point."

Dana lay with arms and legs askew. Her throat looked like something from a butcher's block. An electric carving knife was on the floor by one hand.

"We think LaVerne pushing the door open's what pulled the plug. She, the Esmay woman, was lying against the door. LaVerne remembers hearing a buzzing sound. Had no idea what it was at the time, of course."

The wound in the woman's throat gapped open, oddly intimate. Some secret small thing had squeezed through this portal from elsewhere, leaving our own world forever changed. Beside the wound, to the left, were several long cuts. I leaned down to look closer.

"Hesitation marks," Don said.

"Or signs that she was struggling, turning, trying to get away."

Blood pooled beneath one turned-down wrist. Maybe she'd had a go at that, botched it, before moving higher. Or maybe instinctively she'd thrown that arm up in self-defense.

"Here's the rest." Don turned her head. The back of it, from the crown well into the neck, was cut away. *Scalloped* came to mind. I couldn't remember when I'd last seen this much blood.

"ME says his best guess is she plugged the thing in, took a couple of trial swipes, then pulled it across. Both carotids are gone and she's dead at this point, but there's still ten to twelve seconds' worth of oxygen left in her brain. She's on automatic: her arm and hand keep going.

Then the hand hits empty space and jerks around to the back. Two or three last whacks before she's down. . . . You okay, Lew?"

I nodded.

"It's her, right?"

"Yeah. It's her."

She turns and holds her arms out. Ducking to fit more comfortably, I step into them, hugging her. A low-rider pumps by beside us, bass speakers pounding. Faint strains of Buster's guitar and singing, "Goin' Back to Florida," from inside. Shadows of banana trees move huge on the wall. The moon is full. Then I sense something new. I look up, to the rooftop opposite. The bullet comes to me as I throw my arms wide.

SOMEDAY, I SWEAR, I'm going to put together an anthology, *The Nose Book*. It'll have Gogol's classic story, the nose job from Pynchon's *V*, Damon Knight's "God's Nose" (the universe was created when God sneezed), *Pinocchio*, Steve Martin's tour-de-force nose jokes from *Roxanne*, clips from Woody Allen's *Sleeper*. Maybe I'll put a photo of Mel Gold on the cover.

Leaving the scene on Jane Street, Don and I had gone out for a drink. One drink became two, then four, and I'd finished up, two in the morning, back at the house alone with a half-bottle of plum brandy someone had brought to a dinner party weeks before and had sense enough to leave behind. Vaguely I remembered Verne coming home and trying to talk to me. Not long after, I staggered into the bathroom to throw up. I was lying beached on the front room couch, no idea what time it was, heart pounding, flashes going off behind closed eyes, when the doorbell rang.

I may have opened a closet or two before I found my way to the right door.

"Hi there. Good to see you. Go away," I said, and shut the door.

"Look," I said, opening it again when the bell resumed. I'd meant to say something, had something firmly in mind, but lost it. I may have shut the door again, I'm not sure. Things blur for a while then. Next clear picture I have, we're sitting in the kitchen over toast with melted cheese and mayonnaise and he's telling me how he's just moved here with his family from the Bronx. "That's in New York."

I told him yeah, I thought I'd heard something about that.

"I'm an accountant for J. Walters, an electronics company, been with the firm almost thirty years. No one came right out and said it, but the message was clear. Either I took the transfer, or I'd better start getting my résumé in order. I'm fifty-three, Mr. Griffin—"

"Lew."

"I never did anything else, or lived anywhere else, and I'm fifty-three. What am I supposed to do? It wasn't just me, though. Six other families transferred down with us. We couldn't believe our luck when we found houses all together. Took a while before it sank in there might be a reason for that.

" 'Remember how the real estate agent wouldn't look any of us in the eye?' my wife said when troubles started. Says she knew then that something wasn't right. But I was so determined the move was going to work out, I ignored anything to the contrary.

"It started out slowly enough. Gates left open to let pets out, dirt thrown over walls at clothes drying on lines, newspapers undelivered, trash cans upended in our driveways. Then a couple of us had bricks tossed through windows, what looked like blood poured on our porches. Once again, the message was clear."

"Jew go home."

Gold nodded, then looked quickly to the right and stood as LaVerne entered the room, pulling a robe close about her. Her feet were bare. She beamed a smile in his direction.

"Ma'am."

"Feeling better this morning, Lewis? And while we're on the subject, how did it get to *be* morning already? Tell me there's coffee."

"There could be."

"Soon?"

I got up and started assembling equipment. "Rough night?"

"Rough enough. Not as rough as yours, from the look of it."

I measured coffee into the basket of the percolator and put it on the stove, put a pan of milk beside it to steam. She sank into a chair.

"Mel Gold: LaVerne. Mel's here—"

I turned back. "Why *are* you here, Mel?"

"I didn't say, did I?" Evidently he had some trouble disengaging himself from Verne's smile and that sleepy, soft, cross-eyed look she always had when she first got up. I knew exactly how he felt.

"Not in so many words."

"I told you how it started, how it kept getting worse

and worse. Well, finally it got so bad that my wife was afraid to stay home by herself all day. At that point I went to the police. Problem is, they said, very little's actually been *done*. All of it could be written off as no more than kids' pranks. They'd arrange for squad cars to drive through the neighborhood on a regular basis, every couple of hours say, but for now that was about the extent of it.

"I thanked the officer and asked if it would be possible to speak to his superior. I'd be happy to wait, I said—and wait I did. Finally someone named Walsh came out looking for me. After listening to my story, asking a question or two, he repeated pretty much what I'd already heard. 'But if you choose to pursue this on your own,' he said, 'and that's probably what it'll take, you might want to get in touch with this man.' He slid your card across the desk. 'This isn't coming from me as a cop, you understand.' "

I poured for LaVerne, half coffee, half hot milk at the same time, then for our guest. What was left went into my own cup.

"Just what is it you expect of me, Mr. Gold?"

"To tell the truth, I don't have much left in the way of expectations, from you or anyone else. I just want to be left alone. Lieutenant Walsh said that you might be willing to ask around—'become a presence,' as he put it. That that might be enough in itself. He did mention that you had a wide network of friends."

Did I?

"I've set aside considerable funds over the years, Mr. Griffin. My credit line, you'll find, is excellent."

Not much of a sense of humor, but hey. I looked across the table at LaVerne. She liked him too. That cinched it.

"Assuming I knew what a credit line was," I told him,

"I still wouldn't have the least idea how to go about checking one."

"It's simple—"

"Hey. Relax, okay? I'll look into it."

"Thank you."

I made more coffee and took down details.

AS IT HAPPENED, Mother and Mel Gold departed together—synchronously, at any rate.

She materialized in the kitchen as we were finishing up the interview and second pot of coffee, bags by the front door and taxicab already called, to announce that she'd be going: You don't need me here anymore, Lewis, best be getting myself back home to where I belong.

Mel Gold fairly leapt to his feet when she appeared in the doorway. And when, moments later, the cab blew its horn, he insisted upon carrying her bags out.

I shook his hand at curbside, told him I'd be in touch. He crossed to a mint-green-and-white BelAir.

"Thanks for coming, Mom."

Verne was standing on the porch; they'd said their good-byes inside. Mother glanced towards her.

"That's a fine woman you got there, Lewis."

"I know."

"Don't know what she sees in you, of course."

"Neither do I."

"But you be good to her."

"I'll try."

"Yeah. Yeah, I spect you might do that. . . . You write me sometime, boy."

I opened the door for her, helped her in. She slid forward till she was on the front of the seat, small face framed in the window.

"Two of us are gonna go on loving you no matter what, you know."

I nodded. She slid back on the seat and sat very straight and still as the cab pulled away. She looked like a child sitting there. Small, lost, alone.

That was the last time I saw her alive.

I 've never seen anything like that before."

"Any luck at all, most people never do."

Verne knew about the man I'd killed a few years back, but we never spoke of it, not then, when I climbed into bed beside her after the long drive back with his blood still on my hands, and not now, as we sat together, eleven in the morning, on her narrow balcony. Box seat at the Orpheum. Beneath us opera New Orleans went into its second act.

We all know it's out there, just at the edge of our vision, past the circle of light from our campfires. Camus said only one thing is necessary, to come to terms with death, after which all things are possible; but we go on failing to meet its eyes, ever dissembling, dressing it up in period costume, caging it in music or drama, gelding it to murder mysteries: how clever we are.

How I used to love that late scene from "Benito Cereno." I was fifteen, skipping breakfast before school and ignoring calls to dinner because I'd just discovered books and what seemed to me then their far realer world. Blacks have taken over the ship but with the approach of an official vessel set up an elaborate Trojan-horse masquerade whereby the enslaved whites pretend to dominance.

That to me was the ultimate dissembling. Because the slave couldn't say what he meant, he said something else. And that scene from "Benito Cereno" seemed to me just about as something else as it got.

In African folklore there's a great tradition of the trickster, Esu-Elegbara. Hoodoo turns him into Papa Legba. In America he becomes the signifying monkey, given to self-relexive flights of ironic, parodic language foregrounding what W.E.B. Du Bois defined as the black's double consciousness.

We're all tricksters. We have to be, learn to be. Dissembling, signifying, masking—you only *think* you have a hold on us, tar babies all.

I got up and this time, instead of shuttling glasses in and back out, exported the bottle itself from the kitchen.

"Appreciate your help, Verne. Some comfort in knowing I won't have to disturb Doo-Wop."

"Man's busy making a living."

"Aren't we all."

"But finding her there like that pretty much shuts it down for you, doesn't it? What's left? Eddie Bone's out of the picture. Now the woman."

I drank off the last of my Scotch. Its sudden swell of warmth inside echoed precisely that of the long, slow noon and sun beyond—or my feelings for LaVerne. Front tire flat, her bicycle leaned on its kickstand inches away from my right ear. Before me on the railing were small pots of basil, rosemary, thyme and lemon grass.

"You're right. Precious little left to go on. Clothes untraceable: everything from Montgomery Ward and the like. No mail, of course. Cans of Spam and generic chili, packets of hot dogs; sacks, boxes and condiments from carryout Chinese food, old White Castle burger bags. We're not even sure who was living in the apartment."

The phone rang. Verne went in to answer and remained there conversing, some friend, maybe, or one of her regulars, as I finished off the Scotch. I looked in at her and she smiled, holding out her left hand with thumb, index and little fingers extended: Love you.

Verne leaned against the wall as she talked. The phone was set in a niche there. A table beneath held piles of junk mail and unread magazines, a pad of paper for messages.

Just like the entryway on Jane Street.

Verne hung up, detouring to the bathroom. When she came back out, starting to ask if I wanted breakfast, I'd taken over the phone, was waiting while they tracked Don down.

"Lew."

"What a man. Party all night, still show up for work."

"What the fuck else am I gonna do, stay home and suck aspirin, watch reruns of *Hazel*? How you feeling?"

"Like a garbage bag left out in the sun."

"Good. Hate to think I was the only one. What can I do for you?"

"Had a thought. Jane Street been packed up?"

"Yeah."

"There was a wad of paper on the table just inside. Discarded pages folded in half to make a scratch pad, kind of thing you might jot names and numbers on. Any chance that got kept?"

"Damned *good* chance, if there was writing on it."

"That's what I was hoping."

"Anything there, though, it's already been checked out."

"What I'm wondering now is what was on the back of them, where they came from."

Don thought about that a moment. "You at home?"

"Yeah."

"Let me call down to Property. Any luck, they might actually be able to find the stuff. I'll get right back to you."

While I waited, I went in and ground more coffee. Verne said she was going back to bed. I said I might join her.

"We got half lucky," Don told me. "Most of the papers got tossed—nothing there, Willis said. A few of them had numbers and the like scribbled down, though. Those, he saved."

"And?"

"Five or six of them were mimeographs, announcing a 'town meeting' a couple of months back."

"Where?"

"One of the high-school cafeterias, DeSalvo. In the Irish Channel. Principal rents it out to community groups for a nominal fee."

"Any ID on the group?"

"Nothing but these tiny letters at the bottom, kind of a crooked F with the foot extended to become the cross for a T."

"That's it? You have any idea what it is?"

"Oh, I've got something better than an idea: I've got a cop that just transferred down here from Baton Rouge. Says they started seeing it up there about a year ago, some of the rougher bars. Now they're seeing it a lot. You want, I'll have him call you."

Ten minutes later, he did, identifying himself as Officer Tom Bonner.

"Walsh tells me you're black."

"He tells me you're from Baton Rouge."

"Hey, we all got our crosses to bear, right. How much you know about prison life, Griffin?"

"Less than most black men my age."

His laugh was quick and brittle. "Know what you mean. Wife's black. One of the reasons we moved down here, thought things might be better."

"Are they?"

"Call me back in a year. Anyway, prisons like Angola, you've got the strictest color lines that exist. Whites, blacks, Mexicans and Orientals, they keep to their own, each one's got its own space on the yard, its own section of tables in the mess. People get killed just for crossing the line."

That much I knew.

"Generally all that stays inside. Now it looks like it's been exported, some of these guys have dragged it out with them. Inside, they were dirty white boys, defending themselves in their solidarity against the encroaching hordes, only way they'd survive. Inside, they got religion. Now they're gonna spread the gospel. And the gospel's pretty simple: White's right."

"What's this FT business?"

"Who the fuck knows?"

"So what do they call themselves?"

"Far as I know, they don't. Philosophy seems to be, if you're looking for them, you need what they have, you'll find them."

"They're all ex-cons?"

"That's how it started, right. Real trailer-park types, you know? But then it grew like weeds in a vacant lot. Got every sort lining up behind them these days. Lawyers, ex-servicemen, grocery clerks."

"Police."

"Be a damn fool to deny it. This is America, Griffin. We're all fucking cowboys here. Ride out of town and away, climb a mountain or tower, shoot the bad guys."

"That what they want to do?"

"One, two, or three?"

"Three."

"Yeah. Yeah, what I know, I'd have to say that might be pretty high on their agenda."

I thanked him and he said if I wanted dinner some night, give him a call, he and Josephine didn't know many people here.

My next call was to Papa, who ran an arms and mercenary service out of a bar in the Quarter.

"Baton Rouge, huh? That's Harrington's patch. Haven't talked to the man for ages. Stay where you are."

"Looks like you were right on the one count, Lewis," Papa said when he called back minutes later. "Steady low-end buys going on for well over a year now. Someone's stockpiling for sure. Not the kind of thing B.A.'d get involved with— domestic, which he stays away from, all of us do, and strictly penny ante, small arms mostly—but anyone doing business on B.A.'s patch, first they've gotta clear it with him."

"Who's the stockpiler?"

"No reason he's gonna know that, Lewis, or tell you if he does. Says he can put you in touch with the supplier, though."

Papa gave me the number and I thanked him.

"You said I was right on one count. What's the other?"

"Well, it's not just Baton Rouge. That's where they buy and store, but they've spread out, B.A. says, they're all over. Heard they even had a foothold down here in New Orleans now."

I hung up and went into the kitchen. We'd finished off the bottle. I got another out of the cabinet, poured a glass half full.

Mornings are a time you're supposed to get to start over, shrug off yesterday's cares, engage the world anew. But here I was. LaVerne asleep in the bedroom, the rest of the world going about new business outside, *my* morning still yesterday, yesterday's concerns barking at my heels. I was tired, dead tired, and not a little drunk. Half-formed thoughts simmered to the surface of my mind and sank back.

Real trailer-park types.

Baton Rouge.

I stood there a moment sipping at Verne's good whiskey, looking out the window. Then I found my coat on the back of one of the chairs where I'd left it last night and fished my notebook out of the breast pocket.

I couldn't remember what the differential was, what time it might be in New York, but Popular Publications answered on the third ring and put me through to Lee Gardner. Sure he remembered who I was, he said, I was doing the piece on "the new Village" out in the Bronx for him. Where the hell was it?

I backed up and started over. Reminding him that he'd come to see me in the hospital when he was in Louisiana looking for Ray Amano, and that we'd spoken since then.

Sure he remembered, he said. Good to hear from me.

"I was wondering if you might be able to help me, Mr. Gardner."

"I might be able to try."

"What was Amano working on when he disappeared?"

"Well. . . . He was *supposed* to be working on a new novel, one Icarus paid out a fairly heavy advance on. But like a lot of writers Ray had trouble planning his way around the next corner. Minute he committed to one thing, he'd lose interest in that and find himself fascinated by something else entirely."

"What was the novel?"

"We didn't know a lot about it. The other books had done well, especially *Bury All Towers*, so we contracted for the new one on an eight-page outline. Supposed to be a Grand Hotel kind of thing, individual stories of all these people living in a trailer park. I think Ray actually sent in thirty or forty pages at one point. Not long after that, I had a letter from him saying he was working on something else. Claimed 'the material' had taken him in another direction, that this book was going to shove open doors people had nailed shut. It was going to be important, *big*. In the face of what he'd discovered, he wrote, he couldn't just go on making things up."

"No chance you'd have a copy of those pages, I guess."

"Of course not. They'd be the property of Icarus. I'm no longer employed there."

"I understand."

"You could speak with young Gilden, of course. The new editor."

"I'll do that. Thank you."

"I don't believe I have your address, Mr. Griffin. Per-

haps you'd like to give it to me. Just in case I come up with
something else, you understand."

Next afternoon, a messenger walked up the sidewalk,
rang the bell, and handed over an envelope I had to sign
for. Inside was a note scrawled across the back of a Popular
Publications rejection slip.

> Had bad feelings about this from the outset.
> Ray's as irresponsible as they come, but once
> he bites down on something this hard, it's not
> like him to let go. He'd be at it 24 hours a day
> every day till he dropped—then he'd get up and
> start again, till it was done.

Life stammered on between the time I spoke with
Gardner and the time that messenger showed up. One
thing that *didn't* happen was sleep, but I figured bags under
my eyes and that glazed look (not to mention liquor on my
breath) put me squarely in the PI ballpark. Tradition's
important.

I left a note for Verne, grabbed breakfast at TiJean's,
which is about the size of a trailer bed and serves up red
beans on the side whatever you order, then spent the shank
of the afternoon snooping around Mel Gold's neighborhood, two blocks lined with wooden houses whose sharply
peaked roofs and dark crossbeams made them look like
British country inns shrunk to garage size. Equally diminutive C-shaped yards surrounded them, and they were
in pairs, mouths of alternate *C*'s facing one another across
a common driveway. Well-kept, mostly smallish cars sat
in the driveways. There were clothes hung out on lines in
some backyards.

This island of conformity, order and calm represented
something I would never have, something I'd fled all my

life. Something that (though I could not explain it, then or now) terrified me. These were ghettos no less stark or inescapable in their way than were the city's housing projects, Desire, C. J. Peete, St. Thomas, Iberville.

It's possible, of course, that I only imagined curtains and blinds rippling behind windows as those within marked my progress down the street.

At the end of the second block, everything changed. I thought of science fiction movies in which whole towns were abducted by aliens, plopped back down in the midst of nothingness. You'd see folks standing there at the edge of town, looking out.

America, and civilization, ended here.

It was the sort of abrupt border that a decade or so later we'd get used to, think nothing of, in our cities. Across the street lay a vast empty lot overgrown with banana trees, Johnson grass and sunflowers. It had been used as a dump for appliances, old tires, automobile doors and sacks of garbage. The ground was studded with broken glass. In a clearing beneath one straggly oak sat a cable spool with vegetable crates upended around it. They'd painted a huge red swastika on the top of the spool-table. Dozens of cigarette ends heeled into the dirt. Squashed empty cans of beer all about.

Half a block further along I came across the remains of what must have been a school or church. Time and time's footman-vandals had had their way: it may as well have been an Anasazi ruin.

Another cross street led to the trailer park I'd half expected all along. BAYVIEW BONNE TERRE—YOUR HOME hand-lettered in dark blue on a plywood sign. Had they intended the contraction *You're?*

Behind the trailer park a hundred or so houses roughly the size of the trailers, though nowhere near as well built, had been shoehorned into four square blocks, like tamales in a can.

If the Balkans were the tinderbox of Europe (something I learned in eighth-grade history), then places like this, not a hair different in kind from those I grew up in as a child back in Arkansas, though in today's idiom (we fount some words) *another flavor*, were the tinderboxes America had made for itself.

THAT NIGHT BEFORE she left for work I took LaVerne out to dinner at PJ's, absolutely the best catfish and shrimp around. Sit down and they bring whatever PJ felt like cooking today, always catfish or shrimp in some incarnation: catfish fried, catfish stewed in court bouillon, shrimp creole or etouffé, gumbo thick with okra, shrimp on shredded lettuce with remoulade. I never heard anyone complain.

"This is nice, Lew. Thanks. I needed it."

I poured another glass of wine for me, something from the great state of California. Verne never drank when she was working. She had a glass of sweetened tea. It was big enough to raise tropical fish in.

"You have that look in your eyes, I'm not going to see much of you for a while. That what this's all about?"

I shook my head. She ran fingers lightly down the sides of her water glass.

"How long have we been together, Lewis?"

I didn't know.

"Yeah. Me either. Maybe sometime we'll sit down and figure that out." She reached across and picked up my wineglass, briefly drank. Replaced it. "Be careful, Lew."

Of course.

"And tell me I'll have you back again when it's over."
I told her.

We finished our meal in silence. I took Verne home and spent that night, stoked with quarts of coffee and stale doughnuts from U-Stop, haunting the empty lot and trailer park alongside Mel Gold's neighborhood, watching people come and go inconsequentially.

Eight or nine that morning I was back at U-Stop for a serial refill. Store looked to be the nerve center of the community, like a stargate these people passed through on their way back into the world. They'd ease from the trailer park or houses behind, pull in here for gas, coffee and chatter at the back of the store, maybe a prefab sandwich or couple of doughnuts slimy with sugar, then reenter. Like decompression, for a diver. I did my best to blend in with the wall's beige paint and ignore the sharp looks from those joining me, in jeans and T's, in short-sleeve white shirts with ties and polyester slacks, all men, by the self-serve coffeepot. Should have brought a bucket and mop for disguise, then no one would be taking notice of me at all.

The store had a free bulletin board on the wall by the serve-yourself coffeemaker. It held the usual business cards for car repair, heating and cooling, home improvement, and the usual handwritten notices for apartments to let, entertainment centers, musical instruments, pets and sound systems for sale. One hand-lettered paper read:

FREEDOM.

THE RIGHT TO BEAR ARMS.

First letters a kind of homespun Gothic, tall columns and buttresses all but dripping with blood.

INDIVIDUAL RIGHTS. REMEMBER THOSE?

OR A PIECE OF PAPER CALLED THE CONSTITUTION?

BACK BEFORE THE GOVERNMENT DECIDED *ITS* NEEDS SUPERSEDED *YOUR RIGHTS.*

GOVERNMENT DOESN'T EVEN EXIST—IT'S ONLY THE PEOPLE'S VOICE—SOMETHING *ELSE* IT SEEMS TO HAVE FORGOTTEN.

IF YOUR AMONG THOSE WHO THINK IT'S IMPORTANT THE GOVERNMENT REMEMBERS THIS—SOMEONE WHO FEELS A CALL TO GO ON REMINDING IT—

YOUR NOT ALONE.

I wrote the phone number down in my notebook, glancing up out of habit to record the time as well. 11:12 A.M.

Hour or so later, I watch the messenger climb out of

his van and walk up the sidewalk to the mailboxes. He scans them, and moments later rings the bell outside Verne's door. I take the package inside, pour a large drink, settle down to read. Get up after a while to put on coffee and go on reading.

Ten at night, Jodie shows up at my door. She's thrown him out again but is mortally afraid he'll be back before the night's over—with a load on, as she says. Or with buddies. She's most afraid when his buddies come over. They sit there all night long drinking and after a while (Jodie's words again) their eyes glaze over, like they've gone somewhere else. Things have got a lot worse since he was laid off. And he's been bringing home new friends and drinking buddies that scare her more than the old ones did. He talks a lot these days about inalienable rights, the right to bear arms, what he calls the burden of freedom.

· · · ·

There's no easy explanation: that the world has changed around them, become something they no longer realize, for example. What they're trying to do, it seems to me, is to return to something that never existed, some notion of the U.S. cobbled together out of received wisdom—from old movies, nouns that drop in capitals off the tongue, catchphrases, that call of solitude at the secret heart of every American, the simple demand to be left alone.

· · · ·

They're not heroes, though in another time, and this is part of what I find so fascinating, they might have been. They *want* to be heroes. They want to be heroes all alone, all by themselves, to and for themselves.

. . . .

This is where the world makes sense to me, maybe the only place: looking out the window of this trailer. Out into America.

. . . .

Six in the morning, just past dawn. I'm sitting outside with a first cup of coffee watching herons glide on the breeze, hawks settle onto trees. I look about me—at these trailers with porches or rooms built on, the battered pickups and cheap old cars, at the juke joint just up the road. And realize that I love it all.

Putting the pages back into the envelope, I thought about Rabelais's dying words: *Je m'en vay chercher un grand Peut-être.* I go looking for a Great Maybe.

That's what Ray Amano had done. And I had no idea how it turned out, what he found when he went looking, where he was. I'm remembering forward now, to a time many years later when, like Amano, I'd vanish into my own Great Maybe, book passage on my own drunkboat, walk · off suddenly into Nighttown and come back with dark news.

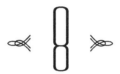

ou boys might not want to do that."

They were only a few years younger than I, but we'd come up so differently the gulf would be unbreachable. I remembered what I'd told Dana Esmay: that we existed in different worlds, that it wasn't like in movies, with secret passageways to get from there to here.

Maybe you *couldn't* get from there to here. Maybe Mother was right: their lives had nothing to do with the one we lived, and never would.

They were, the three of them, pretty much standard-issue Southern suburban white males, dressed in slacks and print shirts over white T-shirts. One, living on the edge, had grown his hair out and wore a small moustache. He seemed to be the leader.

"What the hell," one of the others said, looking not at me but at the moustache bearer. His shirt was yellowish white with rust-colored stains baked into it on trips through his mother's electric dryer, so it looked a little like he was wearing a plate of spaghetti. "Now some nigger thinks he's gonna tell us what to do?"

"What not to do," I corrected him, as the third one shook his head in wonderment. What *was* this world coming to? He'd be the one the others shoved around, gave a hard time, made fun of.

"What is it, man," Spaghetti said, "you can't find enough trouble for yourself back in the projects, you gotta come out here where you know your kind aren't wanted looking for more?"

Moustache took in my black suit. "Shit, and it ain't even Sunday. You one of them Muslims or something?"

I pointed to the things they carried. "Guess I'm not the only kind you don't want."

"It's a neighborhood thing. No business of yours."

"Maybe I'm Jewish."

Since he couldn't decide how to take that, he ignored it. "Those people don't belong here."

"Jews, you mean."

"Shit, man, for two thousand years ain't no one ever wanted them. You think there's not a reason for that?"

"Guess I ought to feel proud, then, since you wanted *my* people. Wanted us so bad you came all the way to where we lived and carried us off. Paid top dollar, too."

"Yeah, and look where *that* went," Spaghetti said.

"No offense," Moustache added.

"Look. You boys have no reason to be here. None of you has met Mel Gold, or any of his family and friends, or knows anything about them." All told, they weren't much worse than others their age, mimicking what they saw around them, filled with frustrations and undirected energies, lightning taking the shortest path to the ground. "Why don't you all just go on back home?"

"What the fuck you think you are, these Jews's bodyguard?" From the look he shot the others, Moustache thought that was pretty funny.

"No. I'm your shadow," I said. "Big black thing that follows you around."

He looked out across the acre or so of dark houses set in regular rows like vegetables in a plot, one of them almost certainly his, looking for reassurance, a reminder of why they'd come here, what this all meant. It wasn't supposed to go like this.

"You boys lay down your burdens and get started now, you can have everything back together inside the hour."

Spaghetti took a measured step towards me. "What you mean back together?"

"Well, I walked in from down there." I pointed towards the stand of water oaks a couple of blocks off. "And as I came by your truck—that blue Dodge back there is yours, right?—I couldn't help but notice as how someone's let the air out of all four tires."

"Damn!"

"I agree. Terrible thing to do to a man. And so far from home, too."

They looked at one another and started towards the truck.

"Boys. . . . Now you won't be needing them, why don't you just go ahead and set those things down right there."

After a moment they did.

I went over and looked. A can of bright yellow paint, some homemade stink bombs, and a sack of fresh dogshit.

About what you'd expect. Just like I'd expected the flyers, with that crooked *F*'s foot becoming the cross for a *T*, in the glove compartment of their truck.

They'd get the tires aired up quick enough, I knew, no problem. I'd also reached around behind the wheel well on the passenger side and cut the ground wire from the starter. It was going to take them a lot longer to find that.

"YOUR PROBLEM'S NOT over, Mr. Gold. It's never that easy. But I don't think the boys will be back, at least. Not *these* boys."

I hung up the phone and looked at the clock. 7:36. I'd wanted to get through to Gold before he left for the office. Verne had come weaving through the door dead tired not long after I had, six or so, and now was asleep, half dressed still, in the back room.

I cracked a third beer and leafed again through the pages Lee Gardner sent me, scanning them superficially at first, like a true believer who's not looking for understanding, for rational connections between words, words and ideas, words and world, but for some subliminal crackle, a *frisson* of revelation. Soon enough, though, as before, I was drawn in.

> Lonnie Johnson, "the brown-breasted black warbler," died this morning. He'd spent the last few days mostly in the narrow channel between wall and bed, but emerged periodically, at first anyway, to rub the back of his head and neck against walls, bedclothes, table legs and people legs to insist that I pet him. He had stopped eating, and began growing ever weaker, until

finally he could barely raise his head. He lay there against the wall, and a far-away, resigned look came into his eye. He was waiting. Urine pooled around him. Last night I got a screwdriver from the cabinet and took the bed's supports apart, so that I could reach down and rub his head lightly. I hope that I'll remember always his gentleness, his sweetness. If another cat came to his bowl, Lonnie would back away and let the other eat, waiting quietly.

I'd turned the TV on for company, a habit I'd taken to of late, God knows why, sound cranked low. Onscreen were four chimpanzees dressed in shiny tuxedos with red bow ties, their bandstand decorated with huge sequined musical notes and the name KONGO KINGS in blue wave-like letters. One chimp sat behind a toy drum set, another at a Schroeder-size keyboard, one held a plastic saxophone, one a banjo. Well trained, they went about their charade precisely, slamming at drum and cymbal, fingering banjo and sax, running hands up and down keys. They were even more or less on beat. Duke Ellington came out of the speaker.

This book, which I'm coming more and more to think of as *American Solitude*, can only end with me alone again, sitting here as at its beginning staring out at strutting blackbirds, a solitary squirrel, the occasional lizard rippling through sunlight. The feral kitten I wrote about back at the first, so many pages ago, became quite tame, in due time moved into the trailer with me, and grew to adulthood.

There is a picture window here (which I

must have mentioned at some point, though I can't remember) almost the exact size of the counter top where I work, a screen upon which the world projects itself. At night, wind catches in the trailer's fissures and faults, moaning in polyphony, sombre Gregorian chants. Alicia writes that she wishes things could be as they were before but knows they cannot.

I recall Santayana's observing that he enjoyed writing about his life more than he did living it.

Around me trees hunch their shoulders and duck their heads like bowlers; a branch scrapes at my window with the sound of a crow's cawing. In this book I will have tried to say many things; others I will not have intended but said anyway, in the simple course of ending one sentence and beginning another.

Out my own window, out LaVerne's, I watched as the day began, people moving from houses to cars, pacing down steps as though counting, stopping at corners to wait their turn, crossing. Mr. Jones did it in the Pinto with a work schedule.

We are all of us astonishing, portable worlds circling and spinning about one another, exchanging bits of matter from time to time like binary stars, our separate lights reaching out feeble and doomed through this darkness we can never understand: we are all diminutive fires.

Diminutive fires. From the Neruda poem I'd quoted to LaVerne back at the hospital. City lights. The diminutive fires of the planet.

I thought of Amano bunkered down there in his house trailer, a squatter, an intellectual passing in shitkicker land, and remembered Edward Abbey in *Desert Solitaire* writing how he'd try having meals in his trailer and suddenly feel the crush of loneliness, how only when he'd moved his meal outside, away from society's trappings, would the loneliness go away.

Hour after hour, day after day, Amano sat looking out his desk-size window at trees filled with birds and squirrels, at one high corner of an adjoining trailer maybe, or the butt end of another, thinking his thoughts of young Joan of Arc, men with no place in the world who nonetheless sense themselves supplanted, slowly dying men and those reborn, great maybes. Behind him a dirt road stretched back to the juke joint on its gravel lot, a borderland of sorts, an outpost, then on eventually to civilization, the city. Around and beneath the trailer he'd inherited from his parents lay lawn chairs with webbing rotted away, cinder blocks whose cavelike hollows housed a variety of small living things, the empty shell of a power lawn mower, two or three garden hoses so long coiled they could not be undone, a terra-cotta birdbath in pieces, hip boots, a galvanized washtub, parts of two outdoor grills.

Day after day he sat there, and in these pages tried to find a way out, to scramble back up the sides of various pits he'd dug for himself. Tried to turn what were essentially journal jottings, stray bits and pieces of his life, into something else, something with form, with substance: fiction, essays, a book. You could feel the need, the pressure of it, lurking and groaning just out of sight, feel even your body's response. But there was nothing when you turned your light that way.

Then three-quarters of the way through, having left behind like a shed skin its labors to become a novel and been swept ever closer to the writer's own daily life, the manuscript changed. Ray Amano emerged from his climb onto the rim of a green plateau.

He had found his theme.

I stood to get another beer and, glancing again towards the window, saw a face there looking in.

"Hosie?" I said from the patio moments later. The paving stones were irregular, kidney and egg shapes, rhomboids, someone's demented idea of a game board. "What are you doing standing out here? Why didn't you come on in?"

His eyes turned to me, dull, distant. Slowly they changed.

"Lew. Didn't know for sure you'd be up. Looked in to see, so I wouldn't disturb you or LaVerne. That was a while ago. . . . I guess I just got stuck there."

"You okay?"

"Get stuck like that sometimes, these days." He shook his head. Things slip up on you when you're not looking. Hard to understand. "Done had a few too many drinks, too. That's the other thing. Ain't much company just now." Language, accent and cadence had reverted to those of his youth. "Not even for myself."

"All the more reason to come in."

He followed me inside and sat at the kitchen table without speaking, not even bothering to pull over the stack of manuscript and check it out, something he'd ordinarily do without even thinking about it. He watched condensation bead up on his beer bottle.

"Lawyers, Lew. What's that line from Claude

McKay's poem? 'While round us bark the mad and hungry dogs.' "

"What lawyers?"

A drop of condensation formed near the bottle's lip, coursed erratically down it.

"They're trying to take my paper away from me, Lew. Say I've got outstanding bills with major suppliers, haven't paid my printer in months, bank loan's in arrears. Now the courts have got themselves involved. I knew all along there was problems, but I never imagined it'd done got that bad. Guess I been letting things slide."

He drank his beer off in two swallows. If it steadied him, affected him in any way, I couldn't tell.

"Yeah, that's what I been doing, all right. . . . They take *The Griot* away, Lew, they might just as soon go ahead and shoot me."

"But nothing's gone down yet, right? It's still only talk."

"Some kind of hearing set for Thursday next week." This from a man who used to untangle the baroquely snarled threads of our city government and lay them out straight on the page: some kind of hearing. He pulled an ancient reporter's notebook out of his back pocket. You could have poured plaster of Paris in there and had a perfect cast of his butt. "I've got it written down. Sorry. I didn't know where else to go, Lew. Who else I could talk to."

Hosie put his head in his hands and for a moment I thought he was weeping. Then I leapt for the trash can and got it in front of him just in time.

"Haven't done *that* for a while," he said, wiping vomit from his mouth. I looked in the can and saw dark blood.

"You get some rest, Hosie. Take the couch out front. I'll make a few phone calls, see what I can find out. We'll talk things over tonight."

I helped him to his feet, offering only what help I knew I safely could, what he'd accept. His body told me when to move away again.

He tottered off into the living room. I sat staring at the window where his face had surprised me minutes before, watching as a bright yellow wasp banged repeatedly against the pane it was unable to see.

"Lew, you come in here?"

I stepped into the doorway. Hosie lay on his back. He'd kicked off his orange work shoes but remained fully dressed. From the way his shirt draped the hollows of chest and ribs I noticed how gaunt he'd become.

"You been looking for some good ol' boys. Kind that don't much care for our sort, got themselves a taste for guns and the like."

"I have."

"You had any luck with that?"

"Don's on it. Some others."

Hosie nodded and closed his eyes. I thought he'd fallen asleep when he said:

"After I thought on it awhile I checked with some brothers I know. Men went through that whole Panther-Muslim thing and came out the other side. Couple of them were there at the Desire projects when the cops came in firing. Still a few old-time hardliners left. Nowadays mostly they stay out of sight. Call themselves watchers. Keep a tally on things that might pose a threat to the community at large, like legislation getting pushed through on the quiet up in Baton Rouge—"

"Or groups of righteous white boys."

"Exactly. Now, since I hadn't seen old Levon for a year or three, we sat awhile and talked. He passed along everything they know, not a lot when you come right down to it. No idea where they might headquarter, for instance—"

"Where they keep their arms stash."

"Or their funds, no. And you know there's got to be a cache of money *somewhere*. Banks being another thing they don't much take to."

"Appreciate the help, Hosie."

"Ain't like they can infiltrate a meeting or nothing like that—is it?" He laughed briefly at the image that conjured for him. " 'But we got our bikes and our chewed-up old cars,' Levon told me, 'and who's gonna notice another poor black man struggling his way home?' Happens one or two of those poor black men came to be struggling their way home right about the time and place these white-and-right meetings of yours were taking place. So Levon says they know two or three of the regulars, since as it happened they were pointed in the same direction as those poor black men. Not where they live. Levon can't give you addresses, anything like that, they couldn't push it that far. But what these men look like, where they hang out—that's a different matter."

He pulled the reporter's notebook from his hip pocket again and held it out.

"It's all written down here, Lew. Towards the back." When I took the notebook, he turned onto his side, knees sticking out from the couch like chicken wings. "Think I'll go to sleep now."

I was almost to the door when he roused: "Lew?"

"Yeah."

"I sleep through till Thursday, you be sure and wake me up."

WHAT AMANO HAD done, suddenly, was shift to the first-person narrative of a white Southern neo-Nazi, an acolyte at the temple, an apprentice. This person relates to us dispassionately everything he sees or participates in, and much of the narrative's power derives from the tension between the two voices going on at the same time in his head, one that of a man lamenting his cat's death and trying to come to terms with the world about him, the other that of a man being trained to contempt, hatred and murder.

> The first one was a skinny runt we picked up out in New Orleans East, near the industrial channel, hoofing it home from a date or dance-hall by the look of his baggy rayon pants and shiny silver shirt reeking of nigger sweat. Robert Lee, he said his name was, though nobody asked him, a real hardcase from the time we dragged him into the van right up till Willard and Dwayne lit into him with meat tenderizers—short planks with handles on one end and nails driven through on the other. He quieted up some then. Toward the end he commenced weeping, his body heaving up the way one will and no tears coming out of him, and he looked up at me and said, "Why y'all doin this, missuh? Ain't I always been good?" And the thing is, I guess by his own lights he probably had been, you know?

· · · ·

Commitment on the one hand to TRUTH (we say what others only think, we become their voice) and on the other to ENGAGEMENT(the struggle will be a long and bitter one, and many of our own warriors will fall) unite us in a bond few others ever know.

· · · ·

"What's wrong? We painted it black for you, honey—black, and about the size you're used to, right?"

Pryor held up the baseball bat like someone who'd just hit a homer. Its blunt end glistened.

"Buy me some peanuts and crackerjacks," LeMoyne said.

"Will you look at that—girl sleeping through the best part. Aluisha. Now what the hell kind of name is that?"

We never gave a shit, but we always wound up knowing their names, they always told us their names—like maybe at the end it was all they had left.

I picked up Hosie's notebook and peeled back pages the same way you would onion layers. The thing smelled of sweat and old booze and looked green with mold at the edges. He'd taken down descriptions of two men—

Tattoo, brush cut, small and wiry but pumped-up, shortsleeve white shirts, sleeves turned up a couple of times.

Pudgy, freckled, overfull lips, "like some twelve-year-old whose body'd shot up to six feet and nothing else followed."

— and, after a large question mark, another:

> Wavy black hair, shiny. Uniform. Security
> guard?

Then I looked at the list of hangouts. A joint I knew out on Gentilly, Tommy T's Tavern, a half-and-half kind of spot, cons and ex-military types in equal proportion. Closer in, in the unreclaimed stretches just off lower Magazine's blocks of shoulder-to-shoulder used furniture stores no one ever seems to enter, the Quarter Moon Grill, a bar so seriously out of kilter that giant alien insects could go in there to throw back a few and never get noticed.

Third name on the list was Studs. The roadhouse by Amano's trailer park.

I stuck a note in Hosie's pocket, left another on the hall stand for LaVerne as I grabbed her keys, and lit out for the territory, up Prytania past drugstores undergoing metempsychosis into bakeries and real estate offices, houses-become-apartments with snaggletoothed, sagging balconies and too many entryways, down a narrow side street beneath the crooked backs and limbs of a thousand cronelike trees, onto River Road, curve of the water an unseen, shining blade beyond the levee.

No way I was going to get into that roadhouse during regular hours, of course, no way I was going to get through the front door at all. Back door and ten in the morning might be a different thing. Our whole lives get handed back and forth through back doors.

Studs reminded me of the barbecue pit my old man built in our backyard when I was a kid, a solid, squat block of ugly glued together with mortar, featureless, windowless, everythingless. It looked more an entrapment, a containment, than a thing in itself, as though someone had said, Nice space! and begun building to hold it in place.

Green Ford F-100 pickup and gimp-framed '60s Dodge in the lot, recommissioned delivery van pulled around back. Ghosts of old lettering showed beneath the van's latest though not recent paint job.

I took off my coat and left it in the car, which I'd parked around a curve further down the road, rolled up my sleeves and scuffed dirt into my shoes. Long before I'd reached the back door, joints loosened and I fell into what I think of as the Walk, a rolling strut that looks carefree and cocky at the same time.

Water steamed in the stainless steel sink, a pot big enough to bathe children in held simmering water and a gelatinous mass slowly dissolving to broth, but nobody was home. I peeked out the pass-through at shoulder level. Two men separated by an empty stool sat at the bar drinking beer from heavy mugs, a line of shot glasses and a bottle before them. One was in shadow, a shape only. His arm passed into light as he reached for his drink, fell back into darkness. The other picked up the bottle, poured vodka into a shot glass, dropped shot glass and all into his beer.

"Sure hope you got yourself good reason to be back here," a voice said behind me.

He was tall and straight and hard and looked the way birches look when bark peels off, skin gray and raw white in patches.

"Yessir. I knocked and called through the door 'fore I came in. I was wondering if there might be work 'round here a man could do. I can clean—do repairs and the like, plain carpentry and plumbing. Cook some too."

"Wardell, that you? Who you talking to back there?"

"Got a nigger looking for work."

"Ways from home ain't he?"

I showed myself in the pass-through. "Yessir. You're right, there. No work back in the ward though, and not likely to be. I figure work won't come to me, I'd best get where I might come across some."

"Now don't that beat all."

"Walk on through that door there," Wardell told me. "Let's get on out front."

"You think there might be something for me here?"

"Yeah. Yeah, I think there just might be. We'll talk about it."

I went through the door muttering my gratitude.

Wardell stayed behind me. I stood by the bar, momentarily invisible, as they spoke among themselves.

"Shit, Wardell, you got any clothes of your own? Every time I see you you got that same damn uniform on."

"I been at work all night, Bobby, like always. You fucking know that."

"Not that it don't look good on you," the third one said, speaking for the first time. He leaned forward into the light. Eyebrows perfect parentheses far above close-set eyes, giving him a vacant, unsettling appearance. His skin was dark, leathery, hands pink and smooth. As though someone else's hands had been grafted on.

"Looking for work, huh."

"Yessir, I am."

"And what would you be willing to do?"

"Do about anything I was able to, I guess. Whatever needs doing."

He nodded. "Get you a beer? Awful hot out there."

"Nosir. You don't have work for me, I'd best be moving along. You do, I'd best get to it."

"Well . . ." He glanced at Wardell there behind me. "Much as I hate to say it, we don't have anything for you, son. Wish we did. 'Cause I admire what you're doing, I want you to know that. Ain't one in a hundred has your spirit, be man enough to do it. You sure you won't have a beer? Take it with you if you like."

I shook my head. "But thank you."

"Where you say you're from?"

"Down by North Broad."

"You done wandered a *long* way off the playground."

Not far enough, I remembered telling Don.

I thanked them all again and, when I turned, Wardell backed out of my way. I went through the kitchen and out, hearing laughter behind me, laughter that came not from any joy or amusement, laughter that came only because it was expected, part of the code.

I returned to the car, put myself back together as best I could, and cut through the trees to the Kingfisher Mobile Home Park and Amano's trailer a mile or so distant. The door was unlocked, just as Lee Gardner said.

Despite the trailer's lived-in look, the man who left here had anticipated being away for some time. Two rooms. In the back one the bed was made, not altogether a common occurrence judging from the state of the bedclothes. Books sat in squared-off stacks, arranged according to size, beneath the bed and against the opposite wall. My eyes picked out *The Conjure Man Dies* and *Blind Man with a Pistol* as I looked over them. An ashtray atop one of the stacks had been wiped clean. In the front room, three or four mismatched plates, a half dozen cups looking to be permanently stained by tea, and a small blue pan, used (from evidence of deposits) to boil water, filled the drainboard. The trash can under the sink held a fresh plastic liner. A small TV in an imitation-wood casing was on with the sound turned low.

I've done it hundreds of times but it's always strange walking into someone's life that way. Here's this person you don't know—and you know however hard you work at it, however deep you scrabble in, you never will know them, not really—yet you're about to enter into this odd intimacy.

Amano's IBM Selectric sat on the counter just as, from his writing, I'd expected, a towel draped over it to keep out dust. His filing system consisted of old typing-paper boxes stacked crisscross. Lower ones had collapsed under the weight, so that the masses of paper inside, not the boxes, bore the whole thing up. A scratch pad of discarded pages folded in half sat alongside, fountain pen centered on it. I picked up the pen. It was British-made, satisfyingly hefty and thick in the hand, not an inexpensive item. The pad's top page was blank.

I got a beer from the tiny refrigerator and started making my way down through the stacks, letters to and from readers, rough drafts and false starts for what eventually was to become *American Solitude*, a handful of short stories torn (didn't he keep carbons?) from magazines with names like *Elephant Hump Review* and *Shocking!*, notes on scraps of paper that meant nothing at all to me (*? 2nd p. grail mcguffin?*).

A couple of boxloads down the stack, there was a thick file of articles and editorials photocopied or torn from magazines, all of it crude and blatantly racist, and atop that, drafts for similar pieces written in Amano's own hand.

Research, surely. He'd done his homework, reading the sort of thing these people put out on a regular basis, then had a try at writing the stuff himself, to get the feel of it, to clamber up inside their heads and sit there awhile looking out.

There could be more to it, of course. Maybe this had been his ticket in, maybe he'd written these hate pieces to gain admission to the group. To prove his candidacy, his right-thinking, or to make himself useful to them.

Or maybe—and the thought wouldn't turn away; I remembered all too clearly the authority of the voice in Amano's fragmentary manuscript—maybe the connections were deeper.

Maybe the connections were authentic.

Maybe led by things seen and heard at the trailer park, from a neighbor like Jodie early on in the manuscript, or at Studs, Amano had started poking about, learning what he could. Curious, appalled, intending at first to turn over the stone, expose what was going on; later, to use it in fiction. But then as he got ever closer he began to find himself strangely attracted. Found himself being taken over by it.

I'd become so absorbed in Amano's papers and my own thoughts that I failed to hear anything until the door lisped open behind me. It sounded like hands being rubbed forcefully together. And when I turned, that's what was there, hands. One in my stomach, hard, the other, not to be disappointed, waiting for my face to come down and meet it.

"Right again," a voice said.

I looked at the canvas-and-leather boot planted on my chest, then further up to close-set eyes and high brows.

"Missing that *hungry* look. Had to be up to something, all the way out here. Old Ellis is right again."

He trod down hard and I heard a rib snap.

Then I went away for a while.

Chandler never wrote better than when Marlowe was being drugged or beaten half to death. Must have been tough out there in La Jolla. Something about British public schools, maybe, so many of them grow up with this masochistic bent.

When I was twelve or so, there was this kid who kept pushing me, wanting to fight. Every day at lunch he'd start up again. Couple of times he even had me down in a hammerlock, but I never did anything. Then one day when he stepped up, before he even had a chance to say anything, I put out my arms, walked him backwards onto some cement steps and started banging his head against them. A teacher out for a smoke ran over and made me stop.

"No you don't. Not that easy, boy." His kick brought me swimming back into focus, coiled around the pain. "First you tell me what you're doing out here. *Then* maybe I let you go to sleep."

He held a knife loosely down along his leg, one of those hunting knives with a massive handle that's supposed to look like a stag's horn.

We both heard it without knowing what it was, a dull slap, the way a board might sound breaking under the bed. He pointed the knife towards me and half turned, listening.

No more.

"Wardell?"

Breath suddenly loud in the room.

Louder: "Wardell?"

He leaned close to hold the knife against my throat.

"You move, I cut."

Stepping to the door, he stood by it, poised, listening. Then reached and pulled it abruptly open. Where before it had lisped, now it screeched.

Joey the Mountain stood there filling the doorway, wearing a dark suit, maroon tie. Pomade in his hair glistened in sunlight. His lapels and shoulders, the creases in his slacks, were architecture.

"What the fuck *you* want?" Ellis said. Holding up the knife. "Where's Wardell?"

Then, that quickly, it was over.

Joey glanced at the knife, and when Ellis's eyes followed his, reached up and grabbed his shoulder, squeezing. Whatever he did hit the nerve there. Ellis's arm went limp; the knife fell. Joey smiled momentarily, then hit him square in the forehead, once, with a fist the size of a chicken. Ellis went straight backwards a foot or so before collapsing.

"Tough guys," Joey said, shaking his head. "Always got to talk to you first, let you know how hard they are, do this little dance. One outside was even worse. Fuck 'em."

He took a couple of steps and looked down at me.

"You okay, Griffin?"

I sat up, managed to prop one arm against undercounter shelving and push myself more or less erect. Joey stepped back as I rose.

"Maybe you oughta try getting to bed nights, not take so many naps." Leg-breaking and stand-up comedy a specialty.

Stand up being easier said than done.

Joey threw Ellis over his shoulder. "Taking this one with me." Seeing he wasn't going to get through that way, he unslung Ellis and held him straight out a foot off the floor, pushing him ahead through the door, a lifesize marionette with broken strings. The security guard lay collapsed at the foot of the steps.

"That one ought to be coming around soon enough. Don't expect he'll waste much time removing his sorry butt."

"Joey, what are you doing here?"

"What the fuck you *think* I'm doing, Griffin. Keeping you in one piece. *All* you tough guys are a pain in the ass."

He started off through the trees with Ellis on his shoulder, walking at a full clip. Might as well have been a raincoat. The dark blue Pontiac would be his.

"You coming or what, Griffin?" he said, never looking back.

I RODE THE tail of Joey's Pontiac back into town, to a deserted dry cleaner's just off the warehouse district, part of our intermittent inner-city ghost town. Tumbleweed blowing past skulls in the street wouldn't look out of place. New Orleans is riddled with these inexplicable lapses: you'll have whole blocks or sections abandoned, boarded up or kicked in, then right next to it everything's fine, commerce carrying on as usual, dragging life along.

Joey got out, retrieved Ellis from the trunk, and came over to my car. When he leaned down, Ellis's head swung forward and banged against the fender.

"Wait."

He started off, then came back: "Someone be with you to take your order soon." He vanished into the building.

Not a creature was stirring.

Well, in truth lots of creatures were stirring. Rats the size of beavers that in other parts of the city took to the trees hunting squirrel; cockroaches that, you cooked them up, they'd serve a family of four; street-smart starved dogs and scrawny cats looking as if every extra day ticked off on the chart of their lives was a victory over holocaust.

Just no *human* creatures. That you could see, anyway. Didn't mean none were there.

And after half an hour or so, one was.

Jimmie Marconi came down the outside stairs from the building's second floor, some kind of office up there probably, in the old days kept workers and management comfortably apart. One of Marconi's men, the wiry one from Leonardo's, followed him, stepping into the recess of a doorway at the bottom of the stairs to become shadow. His eyes peered out at car, street, buildings opposite.

"Here's what you need to know," Marconi told me after he'd got in and sat a moment. "Nothing."

Then he laughed. He and Joey could have worked up one hell of a routine together.

"You do have a way of getting in over your head, Griffin."

I allowed as how he had a point.

"We counted on that."

A kid on a bike came into view down the street and proceeded up it, weaving in slow curves from curb to curb. Marconi's man's eyes tracked him from the shadowed doorway.

Death was the only thing that would ever rush Jimmie Marconi. I sat quietly, waiting till he was ready to go on.

"Funny how Eddie Bone never told you what he wanted, that time he called."

"He said we'd talk about it when we got together."

"Puts you off like that, then he doesn't show at all, sends along this woman instead."

"Looks that way."

"And you still don't have any idea what he wanted."

"None."

Marconi nodded. "Ambitious man, Eddie. Worked hard, took care of business. Good with details."

Yes.

"Ambitious. Always wanted to be a bigger man than he was. Had this whole world of his own, friends, places he went regularly, they'd treat him like some fucking big-shot. You ever see the layout at his apartment, you know what I mean. Nothing wrong with any of that long as he kept it to himself."

Marconi looked around at the seats, floormats, dash. "Nice car."

"My girlfriend's."

"I know. LaVerne. She's fine too."

He smiled, a perfectly gentle, suave smile that put me in mind of carnivorous fish.

"Once in a while Eddie'd do contract work for us. Pickups, deliveries, moving things from here to there. Nothing complicated. Month or so before his death, things fell out so as he wound up holding more of our money than he probably ever should have. But he was dependable—right?"

Marconi watched the kid go out of sight up the street.

"Eddie was okay long as he didn't try to think. Man just couldn't think in straight lines to save himself. Get things all tangled up."

Marconi looked at me.

"I'm telling you this. It don't go any further."

I nodded.

"I don't know what the fuck he thought he was doing. Got it up his ass somehow that he was gonna . . . what is it they're always saying in lousy movies these days . . . he was gonna 'make a difference.' This fucker in his silk suits he don't ever get dry-cleaned, they smell like a goddamn gym sock, but he's gonna make a difference.

"Week or two goes by and we start to wonder. So Joey goes by. Eddie tells him the money's gone. This woman he had at the apartment must have taken it, but he's on her trail. Day later Joey goes back and wants to know how it's going. Good, Eddie says. Yeah, well we know where you been hanging out, Joey tells him. We know what's been coming out of your mouth."

Marconi looked out the window. At one time the building's entire side had been painted with the firm's logo and name. Now only the ghosts of white letters, DY CL N NG, remained.

"This was my folks' place. Started it the year they were married. He was nineteen and she was seventeen. Got the whole thing going on a hundred dollars. What you gonna do with a hundred dollars these days, Griffin? People in the neighborhood said Valentine Marconi could get the stains out of anything—maybe even your soul."

Someone came down the stairs at the side of the building. The wiry bodyguard went over and they spoke. Then the bodyguard started towards the car. Marconi rolled the

window down. The bodyguard spoke softly into his ear and
Marconi nodded.

"We still don't know," Marconi said. He cranked the
window back up. "Maybe the woman took the money, like
Eddie said. Maybe she talked *him* into doing it. Or maybe
it was Eddie's screwed-up idea all along, his pitiful fucking
idea of hitting the jackpot, and the two of them were together on it, accomplices.

"Maybe these dickheads"—he glanced at the stairs,
Ellis up there somewhere, in some condition—"engi-
neered the whole thing. Took the money out from under
Eddie or got him all busted up on their great cause. What
we think is, one way or another Eddie gave it to them."

"To make a difference."

"Yeah. Boy up there didn't seem to want to talk about
it. Thought he was some kind of soldier."

"He's dead."

Marconi shook his head. "Soon."

"You, one of your gophers, killed Eddie."

"It's what happens, Griffin."

"And Dana Esmay?"

"Police say suicide. Why not? Maybe she couldn't live
with what she did, or with what she thought someone else
was going to do once they found her. For all we know, she
had the money, and the toy soldiers put her down for it—
or because she knew *they* had it. We wanted to find her.
Hell, I even asked you to help. And we needed to have a
talk with the toy soldiers, ask them if maybe they knew
anything about our money."

"Which is why Joey was following me."

"Sooner or later you were gonna come across those
boys. You'd find them or they'd find you."

Someone stepped onto the second-floor landing. He held his fist out, thumb down.

Marconi shook his head. "Another tin soldier tipped over on the board. Dead with his toy honor intact. Take care, Griffin."

"Mr. Marconi."

He stopped with one foot out of the car.

"I don't much like being lied to."

"I can appreciate that."

"Or set up. Or tailed."

He shrugged without looking back at me. "Who would?"

The wiry bodyguard came out of the doorway. He stood scanning the street as Marconi went up the stairs, then with a glance my way turned and followed.

It was night now. Streetlights ran long fingers in through the window and caressed the back wall. Neither of us had made any move to turn on lights in the house.

"You missed it all, Lew. I got up and came in looking for you and there was Hosie on the couch making these horrible gasping sounds. That was bad enough, but then they stopped. I couldn't tell whether he was breathing or not. I didn't think he was."

She drank off the last of her coffee. I'd made my way down the first third of a bottle of Dewar's I'd got at the K&B up the street.

"The paramedics said he aspirated—vomited while he was out cold, breathed it into his lungs. There was blood and vomit all over the couch and floor, that really scared me, but they said the blood was probably from his stomach too, that happens with serious drinkers. They hooked him up to monitors, put a tube in his throat, started IVs, and packed him up. The ambulance sat there for half an hour.

All these faces all up and down the street peeking out from behind doors and windows, trying to get a look, find out what was going on."

She got up and walked to the window above the sink, stood there looking out, not saying any more. A banana tree swayed outside, dipping one broad leaf into the air like an oar.

"I'm sorry, V."

She nodded. "I'll make more coffee. Be a long night." When she opened the refrigerator door, light leapt into the room. She took out a can of French Market topped with aluminum foil. Light caught in the foil as she unwrapped it, bounced about the walls, semaphore from signal mirrors far away.

"You weren't here again, Lew. You're never here. All those cases you keep taking on, the Clayson girl, Billy Deacon, that man's new young wife over in Slidell . . . *You're* the missing person, Lew."

She turned to look at my glass. "Can I get you more ice?"

I shook my head.

"I keep trying to tell myself it's going to change, for a long time now. I don't know how much longer I can go on doing that."

She sat at the table to wait. We watched one another. Neither of us said anything. After a while she got up and poured coffee. A passing car lit the part of her face I could see, threw her shadow hugely on the wall.

"Get you anything while I'm up?"

Again I shook my head.

"I wish I could. I wish there was *something* I could do for you."

"You do a lot for me, Verne."

"No. I don't. Nothing that matters. You won't let me, can't admit there are things you need. From me or anyone else."

A moth flew once against the window, went away and came back. Nudged at it again and again, wanting in from the light maybe. In from the cold. Father, the dark moths crouch at the sills of the earth, waiting.

I remembered a story Mom told me, how when she and Dad were first married, living in one of the two-room shacks thrown up twenty or thirty to the block on hardscrabble acreage at the edge of town, this bird, a dove, got in the habit of coming by every morning. First day, it flew into the window and when Mom went out she found it lying stunned in the dirt under the window. She got some cornmeal from inside and piled it up by the bird. Next day about the same time, she looked up and there the dove was, sitting in the window looking in at her. So every morning after that, she'd put cornmeal out on the sill for it. Even after the dove stopped coming, for a week or so she went on putting out cornmeal.

"I've met someone, Lew. An older man, and his life's different from anything I've ever known. Every time I see him it's like visiting another country. But I think he cares about me. I don't know if anyone else ever will, not that much. Or that way."

I nodded. She sat at the table again.

"I have to try this, give it a chance. Give myself a chance. See what might come of it."

"Okay."

"I'm sorry, Lew."

"No reason to be."

"Yes. There is. Good reason."

She stood and dumped the rest of her coffee in the sink, rinsed the cup, set it on the drainboard.

Years later, at an AA meeting, a member told us that just before swallowing an even hundred pills and opening her wrists in the bathtub with an X-Acto knife, his wife had spent the evening—he was out drinking as usual—ironing his shirts. They were in a stack on the kitchen table, neatly folded, when he got home.

"Rent's paid up through next month. You want, I'm sure Mrs. Vandercook would let you take over the apartment after that."

Okay.

"I'll be by to pick up my things later this week if that's all right."

Yes.

"Take care, Lew."

"You too."

When the front door closed half an hour later, I got up and went into the front room. I looked through the records till I found one with Duke Ellington's "In My Solitude." I played it sixteen times while I finished the Dewar's.

"JESUS I'M SORRY, Lew."

Coffee lurched over the side of my cup onto the table. I held on to the cup with both hands and leaned into the table. I'd just told Don about LaVerne leaving.

He'd come by to let me know that Hosie was going to be all right and found me out back on the patio lying up against the fence with glittery tracks from slugs on my clothes. God knows how long I'd been out there or what I had thought I was doing.

I told him what I'd found at Amano's trailer, about my visit with Jimmie Marconi. Then about LaVerne.

"She'll be back, Lew. You guys have split up before, but you're meant for one another. Anything I can do?"

"Yeah." I held up my empty cup.

"Only if you promise to drink it this time instead of splashing it on the table." He poured, then sat. "This other thing, though . . . Have to tell you. You're in over your head on that."

"Marconi, you mean."

Don nodded. "Maybe this other shit too. But Marconi for sure."

"He came to me, dealt himself in."

"So you get up and walk away from the table. You're done playing. Where's the problem?"

"I can't."

"Yeah. Yeah, I know that."

Don tipped his chair back, head against the wall, gently rocking. There were spots rubbed smooth on the wall where others had done that before.

"So Bone hauls ash for Marconi's group and winds up with a bankroll he's not supposed to have. Somehow Marconi's sidemen are so busy they forget to ask him about this. By the time they do, the Esmay woman's in the picture. Maybe she's Bone's love interest, maybe she's running a scam. Maybe both. Then the money disappears. Someone climbs up on a roof and shoots at you and the woman. Bone gets wiped. The woman either kills herself or meets up with an unusually imaginative dispatcher. Meanwhile these self-styled

Aryan types are buying up serious weaponry—with mob money?"

"You tell me."

"And Marconi's dogs are looking to pull them down, make some kind of example of them. One thing."

"Where's the money?" I said. Just what I'd been wondering.

Don nodded.

"This guy Joey the Mountain pulled off of you, this Ellis: you don't think he walked down the back stairs, huh."

"Not with his feet touching."

"So what'd they get from this little episode? They already knew the white boys were in it. This Ellis didn't talk, and you say he didn't, what do they have they didn't before?"

"Nothing."

"So no way they're gonna quit. Not the kind of people that write off their losses and move on. These guys grab on to something, they don't let go."

"But they still have me."

"Exactly. Lonely no more. How well does Marconi know you?"

"Well enough."

"Then he knows you're not gonna lay this down by the goddamn riverside. Figure on having friends wherever you go for a while."

"That's just it. I don't have any better idea than they do where to go. Closed doors and empty bottles everywhere."

"So try rethinking it. They knew about your Nazis—you remember how Tarzan used to call them Nasties?"

I didn't. The only movie house back home was for whites.

"And they knew about the connection with the woman."

"Right."

"What they didn't know about, as far as we can tell, is Amano. Maybe that's the door you have to get your foot in. Maybe there's something else back at this Amano's trailer."

"Whatever's there's likely to be on the abstract side." Like the occupant himself, I thought.

"You able to get any real feel for what that was all about? With Amano?"

"Yeah. I think he went in. Climbed aboard."

"Joined them, you mean. The white boys."

"Right. He was desperate, couldn't find his way into a new book however hard he beat his head against it. Maybe he thought this was the thing that would take him where he needed to be."

"You're saying he went in undercover, like doing re-search. Look around, find what goes down, get the hell out of there and write about it."

I nodded.

"That's one side of the story," Don said. "Other is, maybe instead he goes in, likes what he sees, and sticks around. Winds up buying the whole shitload."

"Possible. He was desperate in other ways too, not just about the book. Kind of person you don't have a lot of trouble thinking he might fall in the odd hole."

"Amano's missing, the money's missing. Chances are good they're together somewhere."

"Makes sense. But I keep thinking about the bodhi-sattva."

"The what?"

"It came up in one of the versions of the manuscript. The bodhisattva. Someone who postpones his own salvation in order to help others achieve theirs."

That's not all I was thinking. I was thinking there *was* something at the trailer. Two somethings. And I was remembering an old saying. If you meet the Buddha on the road, kill him.

THE FIRST SOMETHING was no problem. After five or six consecutive naps during the course of which I became vaguely aware of evening settling in again outside my window, borders of one nap blurring into the next, no checkpoints or crossing guards, I called Sam Brown, formerly of SeCure Corps, now consultant and freelancer.

"Mr. Brown, I was wondering if you could explain to me exactly what this 'consulting' is."

"Well I tell you, it's complicated. But breaking it down to the part a layman like yourself might understand, it has a lot to do with what we professionals call 'billing.' That help?"

"Yessir, I believe that clears it up."

"How you doin', Lew?"

"Few months dumber and poorer than the last time I saw you."

"Ain't it the truth? What can I do for you?"

I described the uniform that Wardell, the security guard out at the trailer, had been wearing.

"Stripe up the side of the leg, right? Like on old-time band uniforms."

"Darker blue, yeah."

"Has to be Checkmate, with that shoulder patch and those fruity pants. Owner's a chess nut."

I thought for a moment he said chestnut, and wondered what new slang had started up. "You know someone there?"

"Lew, I know someone *everywhere*. I'm assuming you need to find this guy."

"As soon as possible."

"Give me his description again. . . . Wavy black hair, shiny. Like Indian hair? Right. Skin grayish white. . . . Got it. I'll call you back."

He did, within minutes.

"Boy's name is Wardell Lee Sims. Been with Checkmate a little over a year, in town a little longer. Used an Alabama driver's license for ID when he applied. With a couple of other agencies before that."

"Why the change?"

"Knew you were gonna ask, crack detective like yourself. You put in about thirty more years, maybe *you'll* get to be a consultant."

"I live for the day."

"Man needs goals. As for that other, let's just say, it comes to security services, Checkmate ain't exactly prime rib. More like frozen hamburger patties, come sixty to the package."

"He was fired from the earlier positions?"

"Officially, no. You call up as a prospective employer and ask 'Is he eligible for rehire?' you get a yes, in compliance with the laws of the land. Perfect attendance. Grooming and general appearance, maintenance of uniform, knowledge of job, performance: all check marks. Everything by the book, right down the line."

"Good soldier."

" 'Cept for this one small area. Here, the silent buzzer goes off. Got some kind of authority hangup."

"Doesn't like it."

"Or maybe he likes it—needs it—a little too much. Lot of times it comes down to the same thing. Maybe he keeps on putting his spoon in the pot and just doesn't like the taste of what he finds. Just a minute, Lew."

Sam turned away to speak to someone. I made out *That takes care of your crisis, right?* just before he came back on.

"First job, Sims threw it over, lasted just under three weeks. Second one, his supervisor put him on suspension, supposed to have to be vetted by *his* supervisor before it became street legal, all academic since Sims never showed up again. Didn't even come in to pick up his check."

"And with Checkmate?"

"Man still needs to learn his ABCs. Starts off on days, within the month he's into it with another guard, he gets switched to deep nights and that's where he stays. In addition he gets hung so far out on the line he may's well be keeping a lighthouse, never see another human being."

"And where's this?"

"*Damn* you're good. Always got the right question. An old factory out on Washington, by the canals. Made canned snacks, whatever those are, and some kind of drink mix, Ovaltine kind of thing, that was big for 'bout a week in the early Sixties. Bellied up a year ago. Only reason they keep a guard is the insurance company tells them they have to, and that's only at night."

He gave me an address and directions.

"I had my friend check the log sheets. Sims be on his third cup of coffee 'long about now. Give the two of you a fine chance to sit down, talk over old times without anyone bothering you."

"Thanks, Sam."

"Any time, my man. Most fun I'm likely to have all day."

I snagged a cab on St. Charles and had it drop me at a Piggly Wiggly within walking distance of the factory. Not much else in the area. Two diminutive humpback bridges Huey Long might have left behind. Some caved-in barbecue joints and the like, one or two corner stores still doing business behind thick plywood instead of windows, a service station halfheartedly resurrected as a God's Truth church.

The factory front was an expanse of glass, hundreds of small panes opaque as cataracted eyes set in slabs of aluminum painted off-white. Over years the thick paint had bubbled up and become pocked, looking encrusted and vaguely nautical. Through one of many panes broken out, I peered inside. Far off towards the rear, beside a worktable, chair and low cliff of shelving heavily cobwebbed like something out of *Great Expectations*, a single light burned. Miss Havisham's dreams, industrial strength.

Around back, all but hidden in banks of electric meters, service panels and zone valves for gas and water, I found a narrow door propped open with a car battery.

Inside, sitting in an ancient desk chair with brass rollers, watching a TV on whose screen faces looked like smudged thumbprints, I found Wardell Sims. His head came around as I entered. His eyes skittered over mine.

"Guess I been waiting for you," he said. "Sure I have. Figured they must of took you when they took Ellis. Either that, or you were one of them. And that whatever it was happened to Ellis, if you weren't one of them, it happened to you too. Figured if it didn't, and you weren't, then you'd come looking for me." He ticked it off as though reciting a syllogism. As though he'd been sitting here working it out in his mind, running it over and over. "I ain't so dumb as I let on to be."

Should I tell him that just that pretense was probably the reason he was still alive—the reason Marconi's boys hadn't come to fetch him?

Onscreen, bank robbers fled down busy city streets with police, both uniformed and plainclothes, in pursuit. Guns fired, citizens exploded from their path. Then, inexplicably, like cats and mice in old cartoons, the robbers turned around, pulled guns, and began pursuing the police.

"What the hell are you watching?"

"Cop show."

"You seen it before?"

"Don't think so."

"You make much sense of it?"

"Not really."

Sims looked up at me with a vulnerable expression. Maybe *nothing* ever made much sense to him. But he wasn't one of the lucky ones: he still couldn't leave things alone, couldn't quit trying. Even if he knew he was never going to get that rock up the hill.

Holding on to the edge of the counter, Sims rocked back and forth, an inch or so, on the brass rollers. His eyes were squeezed shut. Then he opened them.

"I need to come with you, or you gonna do it here?"

He thought I was going to kill him.

I shook my head, and surprise showed in his eyes. Something else he hadn't got the sense of.

He looked past me with eyes unfocused, deep in thought or remembering. A smile's ghost walked across his mouth.

"What do you want, then?" he said after a moment.

I took out a photo of Amano. "You know him?"

"Yeah, sure I know him. Ray Adams."

"His real name's Ray Amano. That was his trailer your friend Ellis posted you outside of."

"That I didn't know."

"He's a writer."

"Yeah. Ellis said. Did some work for us."

"And he's missing. You know anything about that?"

"I know he ain't been around awhile. Used to be, he was there most times we got together, never saying much, just looking around. Always squinted, like someone who ought to be wearing glasses. Whenever he moved, even if it was a small move like reaching for a cup of coffee, he'd kind of bolt, like a badger coming out of his hole."

"Ellis never said anything about why Adams was gone?"

"Not as I can recall. There was a lot going on at the time. Community meetings. Seminars for new people—modeled *them* on Sunday School."

"What did you model stockpiling weapons on?"

"You think we don't have the right to defend ourselves? Got ourselves an *obligation* to do so. Constitution guarantees it. Not that anyone much looks at the Constitution anymore these days. They pick 'em out two or three phrases, ride those right into the ground, ignore the rest."

"Where'd the money come from for those guns, Wardell?"

"Ellis never said. Had a way about him, you'd know when questions wouldn't be welcome."

"You have any idea it was money he'd grabbed off the mob?"

"Well . . . One or two little things I overheard, I had to wonder. You pay attention, things come to you. You get to trying to put them together, make a piece."

"Ellis had the money?"

"Knew how to get it anyway, where it was."

"Not in a bank."

"Not so long as Jews and foreigners run them all, it wasn't."

"What, then? That's a lot of coffee cans, take a hell of a backyard."

Sims shrugged. "Safe, was all he said. The money was safe."

"Was."

"Yeah. Few weeks back he'd arranged to pick up a new shipment after a meeting. My night off, so I was supposed to go along, for the heavy work. He came in to the meeting late, looking equal parts strung out and mad, and told me the pickup was gonna have to be rescheduled."

"He say why?"

"No. And it never was. Ellis started not being around a lot then. When he was, you didn't want to crowd him."

"The money had stopped being safe."

"Pushing the pieces together, yeah, that'd be my guess. None of my business *or* my money, of course. I just kind of figured if it *was* mob money, they'd come and got it, and maybe the next order of business was they were gonna come and get him."

"And if not?"

"Then something else happened."

"But the money was definitely gone."

"No way else to figure it."

He sat quietly, looking off with eyes unfocused, that smile's ghost flitting again across his mouth. He'd finally made sense of something, got this one small rock to the top of the hill.

"So how do we get off this spot?" he said at length. "Where do we go from here?"

"We don't." I walked over and held out my hand. "Thank you for your help, Mr. Sims."

He didn't take the hand, but he nodded acknowledgment.

"You might want to be missing, yourself, for a while. I don't think the mob will come after you, but they might. And there's a good chance things won't be too healthy around your white-boy friends."

Again he nodded.

"One more thing maybe you can help me with. What's the FT stand for?"

"Stand for? Nothing. Ellis told me one of the guys back at Angola, the one who started up the movement there, had FIST tattooed on his knuckles. Typical jailhouse tattoo, done with ink and a pin. Later got his middle fingers bit off in a riot."

Purest form of shibboleth, then.

As I left, on the TV a woman climbed stairs looking nervously about, breasts jutting out beneath her cashmere sweater like rocket payloads.

Outside, street- and headlights were shelled in color, and the night had taken on the peculiar heaviness that always comes before a storm. Out over the lake a few miles away, wind swept its cape back and forth with a flourish, urging the bull in.

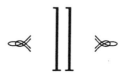

don't know what time it was when the phone rang. Inching towards dawn from the other side. I'd been in bed an hour, two, at the most.

I could hear something pulsing like a heartbeat behind the silence.

"Hello," I said again.

"Are you all right, Lew?"

"Yes."

Silence and that almost-silent pulse flowed back into the wires, a black oil.

"I was thinking about you."

Missing the missing person.

"I couldn't sleep, and started thinking how good it would be to hear your voice."

Ice bumped against a glass. She swallowed.

"How do we ever know what to do, Lew? Where things will lead? What's best?"

"We don't. We make it up as we go along, all of us. Keep our heads down. Then one day we look up and start trying to make the most of what we see, what we've become."

"Never looks much like where we started, does it? Or where we thought we'd end."

"No. It doesn't."

"Could always count on you for reassurance, Lew."

"Probably best that no one count on me for anything. Not when it's all I can do just to haul myself along from day to day. Even then, some days it's close."

"But if we can't count on one another, can't help one another, what's left?"

I didn't answer.

"The world you're describing's a terribly lonely place."

"It is. Yes."

I heard the ice again.

"Take care of yourself, Lew," she said after a moment.

"You too."

Then a moment more of silence before the dial tone caught. I looked out at an orange moon swaddled in layers of cloud and mist like towels trying to blot up its spill.

I tried for sleep, but pretty clearly that bus wasn't stopping here anymore. I sat at the kitchen table, drank a pot of coffee, and watched as morning's hand cleared the window, thinking about LaVerne: how we'd met, our years together. Hadn't ever met anyone else like her. Didn't think I would.

Wallace Stevens was right.

It can never be satisfied, the mind, never.

At the stand-up lunch counter of a service station half a block off Prytania I had a breakfast of grease artfully arranged about islands of egg and of potatoes looking (and tasting) like the fringe off buckskin coats, then caught a cab.

I knew what I was doing: living off the principle of keep moving and it won't catch up with you. Most people, when they do that, they're trying to get away from remembering. I was trying to get away from not remembering, from all those lost weeks, the gulf there behind me. Keep walking and maybe you won't fall back in.

What I *didn't* know was just how much of a fool's mission I might or might not be on.

I thought of Oscar Wilde's "The Devoted Friend":

> "Let me tell you a story on the subject," said the Linnet.
>
> "Is the story about me?" asked the Water-rat. "If so, I will listen to it, for I am extremely fond of fiction."

I didn't know if Jodie existed, if she were real, fiction, or somewhere in between, but since her name came up in the early part of Amano's manuscript, the part that seemed to be taken directly from life around him, there was a good chance she could be real.

Having touched first base with Wardell Sims, I was heading for second.

Portions were not generous. Her name, a few scenes of her coming by Amano's trailer to talk or just to get away after her husband (?) became (verbally? physically?) abusive. He'd stomp around railing at her for hours, or he'd slam out the door into his pickup and be gone all night, or, worst of all, he'd come back half drunk with friends in tow and together they'd go on drinking long into the night, talking about their rights, how niggers were taking their jobs, and how things had to be put back in place again, way they were meant to be.

One entry contained a brief description of the woman he called Jodie. No way of knowing whether this might be any more or less fanciful than the name, or, for that matter, the character herself. Maybe he'd made them all up, person, name, appearance, or had embroidered the details past recognition, like blowing up rubber gloves into fantastic rooster's combs. But it was worth a try.

I started off with the trailers close by Amano's. At the first, no one was home, or had been home for some time, judging from the mass of handbills jammed into the doorframe. At the second an elderly woman came to the door in walker and hightop tennis shoes and said that yes she lived alone here now since Max passed on six and a half years ago and not a day went by but she missed him, meals were the worst so she didn't eat much anymore.

Third pass, I flew low over a woman who I hoped (surely they couldn't be all hers) was running an illegal daycare center.

Fourth and fifth stops got me variations of TV Blaring With _____ (Husband Wife Son Daughter Other) Shouting Above The Din To _____ Offstage.

Women in housecoats or print dresses gone perilously thin. Guys in underwear shirts and pants with buttons undone at the waist, accessorized with beer cans. Young kids taking care, shepherdlike, of younger ones. A gloriously drunk late-middle-age man in corduroy suit gone shiny with wear, narrow yellow knit tie, blue shirt frayed to white threads at the collar; he answered the door holding a copy of Dunsany's *Last Book of Wonder*.

"My husband's not here," the woman said at my

twelfth or thirteenth stop. She'd barely got the door open before she said it, and I had the feeling she said it a lot: to bill collectors, rent collectors, collectors for the *Times-Picayune*, postmen needing three cents additional postage on a letter.

Brownish-blond hair pulled back in a thick braid, like a loaf of fine bread. Small, perfectly formed ears. Eyes close-set, scar from a childhood accident bisecting one eyebrow.

"I'm looking for an old friend," I said, "Ray Adams," watching for the reaction. I wasn't disappointed. "It might be better if I came in."

She withdrew from the door and stood with her back against a closet, giving me just enough space to squeeze inside.

"Yeah, okay," she said.

The description hadn't included the cicatrix jagging down her jawline and neck, but then, that was recent. She wore oversize shorts and a white blouse with long sleeves, no shoes. She looked as though she'd gone to bed a little girl and woke up forty years old.

"I don't have anything to offer you. Coffee or anything, I mean. Bobby forgot to give me money. He meant to."

Momentarily I wondered: meant to give her money, or meant to forget? And was her putting it like that a form of subversive aggression? Maybe this woman, too, knew something about dissembling, how it lets you strike out without seeming to, how it lets you go on.

"That's all right."

Then she realized that I was waiting for her to sit before I did, and looked embarrassed by it. She dragged a chair over from the dining nook. I sank into, decidedly not onto, the couch. It was covered by a throw, a fits-all dark paisley cloth reminiscent of bedspreads, full of folds and creases like time itself. Things cellophane- and crackerlike crinkled and crackled under me. I peered at her through my own peaked knees as through a gunsight.

"You knew about Ray's . . ." What *was* the right word? ". . . masquerade."

She nodded. "And you know Ray?"

"To tell the truth, I haven't met him. I *am* looking for him, though. I was hoping you could help me with that."

"You said you were his friend."

"I did. I said that. Is your name Jodie?"

"Josie. From Josephine, but nobody calls me that. What are parents thinking when they give names like that to a kid? Josephine, that's someone with a handful of rings wearing one of those, what do you call it, those flowery tent things—muumuus. So you call yourself Jo. Names don't get much plainer than that, what kind of life are you going to have?"

She stopped herself and looked around without any seeming awareness of the irony of what she'd just said. I had the sense that her chatter didn't come from nervousness; that this was simply the way her mind worked and she allowed it to go on doing so in my presence. I also had the sense that she'd made that choice.

"Josie."

Her eyes came back to me. "Yes, sir?"

"When did you last see Ray?"

"It's been a long time. Is he all right?"

"I don't know. That's part of what I'm trying to find out. You have any reason to think he might not be?"

She glanced at me and almost immediately away again.

"I've been thinking about getting new curtains. Add some color, brighten things up." We sat together looking at the weightless, paper-thin aluminum frames, curtains like the windows themselves curiously foreshortened, dwarfish, out of proportion. Pictures of teakettles and potted plants on them.

"Were you and Ray close, Josie?"

"I guess. I couldn't say anything to Bobby, naturally. But Ray was always there. Any time day or night, his light would usually be on. I got lonely or scared, all I had to do was walk over and sit down, talk to him. At first he just listened, being nice. But when I started talking about Bobby's new friends, I could see him getting interested. I wasn't ever sure why."

"These were the guys talking about their rights?"

"Their rights, and how they were always being kept down. Like they knew squat about being kept down—you know what I mean?"

"Yes. I do." I remembered Himes's identification, as a Negro, with women, and at the same time how terribly he could treat them.

After a moment, she nodded.

"This was the first Ray knew of them?"

"I think so. And at first he didn't say much, but I could see the change come over him whenever I mentioned Bobby'd had some more of his friends by again. Like a light started up behind his eyes. Though he'd never bring it up unless I did. So I started paying attention when they were around, trying to remember, and I'd tell Ray about them, stories they told, things they said. Eventually that was almost all we'd talk about. I was kind of sad about that, but it made Ray . . . I don't know if happy is the right word."

"He never told you why he was so interested?"

"Not in so many words. Like I say, he started asking questions, where Bobby met these friends, what they looked like. Sometimes I'd go over and he wouldn't be in his trailer, he'd be up at Studs, though he hadn't ever gone there before. He didn't even drink before that, that I know of. One of the last times I did see him, he told me if ever I came across him anywhere else, I should act like I didn't know him. He said don't be surprised if whoever he was with was calling him Ray Adams."

"You saw him after that, though."

"Yes, sir. Twice. The first time, it was early morning, eight or so I guess. Bobby'd just gone to work, anyway. Ray came to the door and said he couldn't talk right now, he was writing. Before, he'd always stop what he was doing when I came over, like nothing else mattered. I sure wish I had something to offer you. No one ever comes here much except it's with Bobby. I'm sorry."

I told her it was okay.

"The last time, it was two, three in the morning. I was up watching TV because Bobby and I'd had a fight and I couldn't sleep after he'd roared off. Some movie about a woman getting even with men who'd abused her, searching them out one by one and killing them, but then she falls in love with the cop who's searching for *her* and gives it all up. *Taking Care*, something like that. In the middle of it, Ray shows up. He's just there, suddenly, in my window. I almost pee. 'Bobby's gone, right?' And when I say yeah, he is, he comes on in.

"He tells me he may be away for a while. Says he wants me to know how much talking to me, 'our friendship,' has meant to him over these past months. I never had a man call me his friend before. I made him drink a cup of coffee with me—I remember I had to add some instant to what was left in the pot—and said I sure would miss him.

" 'I want you to have this,' he said. 'You ever need to get away from here, it'll be there, you don't hesitate to use it.' And he handed me a key. All the time I knew him, Ray never once owned a car. But now he'd gone out and bought one, an old Ford Galaxie, he said, red, with those wing-looking things on the back. Had it parked in the lot behind a garage a mile or so from here."

I asked if I could borrow the key and she told me she didn't see why not.

At the door I thanked her.

"Maybe I could come back later and speak to your husband," I said. "I wouldn't let on that I'd already talked to you, or say anything about you and Ray."

Her eyes went to a spot inches beneath my own, touched down lightly and were off again. "You might come back again sometime?" She smiled. "No, of course not, why would you? Bobby's gone too," she said, "over a month now."

When she'd told me Bobby forgot to give her money, I naturally assumed she meant this morning before he left for work. Over a month ago. She'd been living alone, without money and without much of anything else, treading water, all this time.

"I'm sorry."

"It's all right. I never could hold on to a man," Josie said.

WE NEVER FOUND Ray Amano, or any further trace of him. What I did find, in the trunk of the Ford, was a nylon gym bag stuffed with money and a complete manuscript of the novel he'd been working towards for so long. Hosie serialized it in *The Griot*; Lee Gardner, then editing for David Godine up in Boston, published it in book form under one of several alternative titles scribbled in pencil on the first page, *Verge*.

It tells, as you'll recall, the story of an unremarkable man who has moved into the trailer his parents left behind at their death and goes about his shuttle from home to work to restaurant or bar with no suspicion there could be more. Early in the book, in fact, he tells us that sometimes he thinks of himself as transparent, thinks that others are finding it harder and harder to see him, and that he lives "accidentally." Then one evening a woman named Jodie sits beside him at a diner where he's having coffee. They talk for a while, saying nothing much of particular import. They part, and as he stands motionless by his locked car, for a moment he cannot remember what is supposed to come next, finding the proper key, fitting it to the lock, turning. He realizes that he feels something wholly new; for the first time in his life he feels, feels it physically, the possibility of *more*. The sense of it comes to him at once as a fullness, a kind of tumescence, and as a lack: something missing within him. Eventually he connects with a group of stark, hard-ridden men who do not so much express things he knows within himself and cannot verbalize as they express sentiments that give tentative shape to the swelling emptiness. With the first death he witnesses, that of a young black man picked up beside the road in New Orleans East, he realizes that he is becoming visible again. I am at the verge, on the sill, in the doorway, he writes. Look at me. Now, he says—now and from here on, I live deliberately.

In the time since, sitting first in LaVerne's kitchen, then in Amano's trailer, I'd read those early, fumbling starts, Amano's book had gone on shedding skins, a new animal each time it emerged. Every line, every sentence, every scene or thought had been worked over, revised, slashed at, in some strange sense *purified*, to the point that reading it became a kind of physical assault. Amano had figured out that we gon be here a taste. Singing in that other language, he had fount some words.

Chekhov insists that once a story is written we cross out the end and beginning, since that's where we do most of our lying. What you have here, then, is all middle: all back and fill, my effort to reconstruct the year missing from my life, to hold on to it.

I sat for a long time in Amano's trailer that day, looking at the lumpy nylon bag and the manuscript on the counter before me, trying my level best to imagine, to reinvest, this man's life—much as, in weeks to come, I would begin trying to retrieve my own.

Anonymously, through Hosie, I would turn most of the money over to The Black Hand, a onetime militant group whose roots had spread widely and deeply into community service. Black Hands done become black*smiths*, Hosie said. Forging in the smithy of their souls the uncreated conscience of our race, and so on. The rest of the money, Josie would discover just inside the door of her trailer one morning.

I would see to it that Lee Gardner got Amano's manuscript.

I would also, in those following weeks, have a final conversation with Jimmie Marconi.

We sat on a bench in Jackson Square as early-morning

sun struck the face of the cathedral across from us. People with hoses out front of shops all over the Quarter now, washing down sidewalk and streets. Delivery trucks rumbling up like camels at market to discharge their wares.

"Probably not one to get up early, are you?"

I shrugged.

"Neither was I, not for years. Something about it, though. Something in our body, connects with seeing that new sun, watching how the world changes."

A pigeon bobbed up to him and pecked at the toe of his shoe. The pigeon itself was the color of old-fashioned two-tone shoes, brown and white. Marconi watched it.

"World changing more than we want it to these days. Like it's always trying to catch up with itself and never can."

Marconi looked down again. The pigeon went on pecking.

"Funny how the money never turned up," he said.

"You never know."

"Yeah. Sometimes you don't."

Marconi watched me, expressionless. When he stood, the pigeon strutted away, dozens of others sweeping out before it, left to right, in a slow wave.

"Bullet was never meant for you."

"I thought as much."

Marconi nodded.

"Any connection we once had, any kind of debt or understanding, it's over now, Griffin—you understand? It's settled."

LaVerne would go on calling for a while, every few days, late at night or halfway through, at three or four in the morning. Then she'd stop. Slowly sinking (though I didn't know it at the time) into her own very private slough. Once I saw a sign spray-painted on the side of a 7-Eleven: Convenience Kills! So does hope.

What are any of our lives but the shapes we force them into? Memory doesn't come to us of its own; we go after it, pull it into sunlight and make of it what we need, what we're driven towards, what we imagine, changing the world again and again with each new quarry, each descent, each morning.

I was thinking of Chandler that day as I sat looking at the lumpy nylon bag and Amano's manuscript.

Rain smashed headlong against the panes. The trailer shook with the force and fury of it, as though something pushed at the borders of the world, about to break through.

Did I have some presentiment of what was coming as time inched further along on its glittery tracks? Looking back now, I think I did, that I must have; that somehow I saw in those beginnings the ghettos we'd gather towards in years to come, gangs of children hunting the streets set against one another and themselves, the myth of equality mugging and rolling its eyes and smacking rubbery lips everywhere I looked, everywhere. But I know that much of this, perhaps all, is only memory, only what I have witnessed since then seeping back like a stain into the past.

American society has set us against ourselves, just as Himes said, just as he said over and over again till no one wanted to hear it anymore if they ever did, but I guess our self-destruction hadn't moved ahead fast enough to suit people like Ellis, Bobby and Wardell Sims. We just couldn't get *anything* right. However patiently and persistently and loudly it was explained to us, however much rope we were given. We weren't getting the job done, weren't destroying ourselves fast enough, so they, people like Ellis and Sims and these other white boys, were going to help us. I didn't want to think how ugly it was going to get.

So that day I sat there by the gym bag of money and the manuscript in Amano's trailer with the roar in my ears, watching rain dissolve the outside world and thinking how Chandler had ended *The Big Sleep*: "On the way downtown I stopped at a bar and had a couple of double scotches. They didn't do me any good."

I tried anyway.